"I'm a patient man, Katelyn. Usually. But there are some things I have trouble waiting for."

"What do you have trouble waiting for, Luke?"

"This." He leaned closer, his eyes intent, and took her chin in his hand, running his long fingers from the curve of her jawbone to the curve of her chin. Gently he drew her face to meet his own and lowered his lips to hers. The heady, masculine smells of leather, horseflesh, and musk hypnotized her. His lips, dry from the gusty breezes and pounding sun, traced a pattern across her own, eking from them the very response she had vowed not to give. She surrendered and leaned forward, carelessly jeopardizing her perch on the top fence rail.

"Delicious." He pulled away, smiling, licking his lips as though he had just tasted sweet wild honey. "I had good reason to be impatient."

Dear Reader,

The Promise Romance® you are about to read is a special kind of romance written with you in mind. It combines the thrill of newfound romance and the inspiration of a shared faith. By combining the two, we offer you an alternative to promiscuity and superficial relationships. Now you can read a romantic novel—with the romance left intact.

Promise Romances® will introduce you to exciting places and to men and women very much involved in today's fast-paced world, yet searching for romance and love with commitment—for the fulfillment of love's promise. You will enjoy sharing their experiences. Most of all you will be uplifted by a romance that involves much more than physical attraction.

Welcome to the world of Promise Romance® — a special kind of place with a special kind of love.

Etta Wilson

Etta Wilson, Editor

Dakota Dream

Judy Baer

Thomas Nelson Publishers • Nashville • Camden • New York

Published in Nashville, Tennessee, by Thomas Nelson, Inc., and distributed in Canada by Lawson Falle, Ltd., Cambridge, Ontario.

All of the nonhistorical characters and events in this book are fictitious. Any resemblance to actual persons, living or dead, or to actual events is purely coincidental.

Scripture quotations are from THE NEW KING JAMES VERSION of the Bible. Copyright © 1979, 1980, 1982, Thomas Nelson, Inc., Publishers.

Promise Romances and colophon are registered trademarks of Thomas Nelson, Inc.

Printed in the United States of America.

ISBN 0-8407-7389-7

For Sandy Huseby and Kathy Eagle
My supporters, cheerleaders, and valued friends.

ACKNOWLEDGMENTS
Thanks to the North Dakota State Library and its
staff, who willingly and unquestioningly sent me
information and answers to my inquiries, no
matter how odd or inconsequential they
seemed. My research could never have been
done without them.
And special accolades to Medora, North Dakota,
for being the charming, thought-provoking place
it is.

PROLOGUE

Medora
1883-present

Medora, historical hub of the Dakota Badlands, thrives today on tales of yesterday's heroes, not the least of whom was a French nobleman with an eye to the throne.

Antoine de Vallombrosa, Marquis de Mores—French aristocrat, North Dakota cattleman, valiant swordsman, tender and faithful husband—captures the imagination. Forever haunting the wild and sinister Badlands he once claimed, he still influences the lives of those living in the shadow of his empire.

The Sioux called this land "Mako Shika" or "land bad," for they believed the terrain to be inhabited by evil spirits. French trappers and explorers and settlers elaborated, calling the territory *mauvaises terres à traverser* or "bad lands to travel over." Hence, the Badlands earned a little-deserved reputation for robbers and desperados seeking refuge in the twisted hills.

Captivated by the idea of financial speculation fused with grand adventure, de Mores focused his attention on the Badlands of the Dakota Territory in 1883. Despite its reputation, he dreamed that the hamlet Little Missouri would become the beef slaughtering capital of the Northwest, providing him the means to validate his claim to the throne of France.

When Little Missouri proved unresponsive, the im-

7

perturbable marquis founded another town on the opposite bank of the Little Missouri River. Breaking a bottle of champagne over a tent peg, he christened the place Medora for his vivacious titian-haired bride, Medora von Hoffman.

It was to this settlement that Theodore Roosevelt came. He traveled from the lap of luxury to the primitive Badlands to seek his health and lose himself in the rigors of Western life. Roosevelt also influenced the life of the little cowtown, imprinting Medora with his qualities of honesty, loyalty, and compassion.

While Roosevelt's Badland experience eventually led to the presidency, de Mores' sojourn in Medora led to personal and financial disaster. His confidence and keen insight could not overcome the collusion between the railroad magnates and the Eastern beef trust. Their verbal criticism, false advertising, and sabotage shattered de Mores' dream.

Beaten, but not humbled, de Mores left the Dakota territory in 1886 to conquer new lands. With his departure, the town of Medora withered and shrank. All but a few dozen people moved, some even taking their homes with them on flat cars. Only a few hardy souls remained, but they were enough, for Medora flourishes again today, a tribute to the marquis and his contemporary, Theodore Roosevelt.

Chapter One

Katelyn Ryan stood before the Chateau de Mores, straining to see its sprawling outline in the moonlight. Her red hair was but a glint of russet in the darkness.

Though she'd returned home from Chicago only hours before, her first impulse was to climb the dusty bluffs to the Marquis de Mores' summer home. The museum was closed for the night, but she'd found her way past the bolted gates at the bottom of the hill. Here in the shadow of the chateau she had whiled away many hours in her youth, enthralled with imagined exploits of the colorful marquis in the mansion as it had been a century before.

Even now she could conjure up her childhood image of him—a straight, proud man with lean, muscled thighs that gripped the burnished leather of his saddle. His western hat, pulled low, concealed a patrician forehead and dark, enigmatic eyes. After all these years and all the pain she'd endured, Katelyn was still intrigued by the man who could build such a mansion in these savage and mysterious hills and cast it off when his interest waned.

Grinning, she chastised herself for her overactive imagination and edged her way closer to the building.

She loved Medora's tales of derring-do. Even at twenty-six, she could evoke a lifelike image of the marquis on the land he'd once called home. That was part of Medora's charm—and more than a fraction of why she'd returned.

As Katelyn raised her eyes from the steep incline, her breath caught in her throat. On the dark horizon at the crest of the butte a rider had appeared, a centaur etched in moonlight.

It was as though the marquis had come to life. Spellbound by the apparition, Katelyn stood unmoving as the horseman reined toward her, coming quickly with the muffled clatter of thudding hooves on dry, flinty earth.

With surprising grace the rider swung from the saddle, sweeping the hat from his head to reveal a dark crown and a dark slash of moustache on his upper lip. His hand, casually resting on the rifle in the saddle scabbard, heightened the illusion. Whoever this nightrider was, he even *looked* like the marquis!

Fingers of apprehension skittered through Katelyn as her city instinct came to life. She was alone on the hillside with this stranger whose hand rested so familiarly on his gun.

Then, in a voice rich, soft, and singularly pleasant, but with a bite of metal beneath the even tone, he began to speak.

"What are you doing up here? This area is closed to the public except during the regularly scheduled hours. I'm afraid you're trespassing, madam."

Katelyn suddenly regretted her impulsive visit to the chateau. But she had as much right to the hilltop as...as whoever this was!

Squaring her chin and restraining her red-haired temper, she retorted, "I didn't mean to trespass. My fa-

10

ther said it would be all right to come. I'll be working here soon." She emphasized each assertion with a step toward her inquisitor.

But the dignity she'd mustered was quickly shattered as Katelyn's ankle twisted on a sharp outcropping of rock. She fell, sprawling down the hill's incline and landing hard on her backside, head below, feet waving wildly above.

A chuckle floated down to meet her.

His laughter was simply too much. The weariness of a long day's drive and the maelstrom of emotions that had brought her back to Medora left her no energy for a confrontation.

Ignoring his outstretched hand and the sound of his voice calling to her across the barren slab of the bluff, Katelyn scrambled to her feet and ran, skidding and slipping toward the lights of Medora and her parents' home.

Relieved to find the light out and the screen door unlatched, she slipped into the familiar house. Tiptoeing into the cozy, cluttered bathroom, she punched the lock on the door and slumped onto the tub's broad rim, holding her head in her hands. A sizzling burn licked its way upward to her cheeks.

Caught trespassing! How foolish she must have looked to the man on the hill! His laughter still rang in her ears. Clamping her hands, palms inward, to the sides of her head in a vain attempt to muffle the memory of his laughter, she shook her head in dismay.

"I should have waited until morning to see the chateau," she announced to a school of fish swimming across the bathroom wall.

In her absorption with Medora's colorful past and the century-old charm of the chateau, she'd imagined for a moment that the enigmatic man on the bluff was the marquis. Had that night watchman known her mind, he'd have had more reason yet to be amused!

She managed a sad, ironic smile. Perhaps the last few weeks had taken an even greater toll on her emotions than she'd suspected. Randy Baker had left her a malignant legacy. Of that there was no doubt.

Putting the embarrassing incident from her mind, Katelyn sought relief under a hot, pelting shower. Some minutes later she stepped out, her auburn hair darkened by the moisture, and stood before the bathroom mirror.

Turning sidways, she recalled the evening's events. On her hip a dark and angry bruise was spreading, an aching reminder of her clumsy tumble.

Stung by the memory, she grabbed for her fleecy robe and shrugged it on, knotting the belt in uneven jerks. But as she slipped into her childhood room, the humor of the situation began to tug at her consciousness. A smile tweaked her lips as she pulled a silky nightgown over her damp skin and roughly towel-dried her auburn curls. And then, remembering her bottoms-up position on the hillside, she grinned broadly.

"I guess I got what I deserved," she commented aloud. The incident nearly forgotten except for the stiffness in her hip, Katelyn gratefully slipped between fresh, sun-dried sheets. With the smell of dry grass and fresh Dakota air in her nostrils, she slept.

But all through her dreams that night rode a tall, dark man, gun in hand, laughing as she attempted to escape from him.

The eastern sun filtered through parted drapes and shone directly onto Katelyn's crumpled pillow. Restlessly turning her head from side to side, she struggled to escape the glare. Finally, she willed herself awake, stretching and curling. She dropped one leg from under the covers and over the rim of the bed. As she threw back the blankets, the morning air cooled her sleep-warmed skin.

With one glance at the disheveled pile of clothing on the floor, the embarrassing adventure of the night before came rushing back upon her.

"Well, Katelyn, old girl, worse things have happened to you," she commented to the oval mirror above her dresser, "much worse…"

Fighting the persistent thoughts of her former fiancé, Katelyn willed away the pain and hurt. Perhaps she should be grateful for the episode on the hill. That unexpected marquis look-alike had wiped thoughts of Randy Baker from her mind for an entire night—the first in many weeks.

With a determined set to her jaw, she tugged on a pair of slim-fitting jeans and a body-skimming cotton T-shirt of robin's-egg blue. Wrapping a hand-tooled leather belt around her slim waist and clasping the silver buckle with its turquoise stone, she turned to the mirror to brush the tumble of auburn hair cascading about her shoulders.

Katelyn emerged from her room just as her mother, still rosy from sleep, stepped into the hallway.

"Up already? I'll go start breakfast!" Mrs. Ryan eyed her daughter in sleepy amazement.

"Don't bother, Mom. It's only three blocks to the Rough Rider Hotel. I'll have something there." She pecked her mother's cheek and called back over her shoulder, "Don't worry about me. I'll be home later."

She pushed open the screen door and stepped into the crisp morning air. Cool and invigorating, it slapped Katelyn's cheeks to a healthy glow. The scent of frying bacon from the kitchen next door made her mouth water and her step quicken. It *had* been wise to return to North Dakota, she decided. This was the place to replace her memories of Randy with happier thoughts.

History had left its mark on the little cowtown. The Marquis de Mores would have been pleased to see his slaughterhouse and packing plant standing as a living memorial to his ingenuity. The abattoir smokestack, all that remained of his grand dream, loomed over the city.

Katelyn's step quickened as she neared the hotel, her boots clattering on the rough board walk. The Rough Rider had been named for Theodore Roosevelt's cavalry regiment in the Spanish-American War and had been built in 1883, the year de Mores arrived. Now it was completely restored, standing as it had a hundred years before, ready to comfort weary travelers within its rough board walls.

"Well, welcome home, stranger!"

"Arne! Jean! Hello!" Katelyn's oval face beamed at the sight of her long-time friends, and her hazel eyes shone with affection.

"Pull up a chair and have some coffee. Here's a cup." Arne dangled the mug from the tip of his meaty forefinger.

Katelyn scooped the cup away and poured the steaming black brew. She held it to her lips and savored the aroma. Even the coffee was better in Medora.

"Well, aren't you going to tell us about life in the big city?" Arne interjected. "Did you miss us, kitten?"

"More than you'll ever know," Katelyn laughed. "Thanks, Arne, for holding my job open for me." Katelyn squeezed his thick forearm in appreciation. "I knew Medora wouldn't let me down."

"A purely selfish move on my part, my dear. You're the best tour guide the chateau ever had. You know more about the Marquis de Mores than he knew about himself!"

"Probably," Katelyn laughingly agreed. "I always was fascinated by him when I was a teenager."

"Have you outgrown it yet?" Arne inquired, a smile lifting the corners of his lips.

"Almost. It's still a glamorous story. A rich, handsome marquis bringing his family to the middle of the North Dakota Badlands to launch a cattle empire. Naming a town for his wife Medora. Building her a mansion. Then leaving to build a railroad across Indochina. It's the stuff of fairy tales." She grinned. "You know you two are as intrigued by Medora's history as I am."

Jean chuckled her agreement. "It's catchy, this living in a historic place, re-creating the past for tourists. I'm delighted you came back for the summer. It *is* just for the summer, isn't it?"

Katelyn's breath caught in her throat. "I think so. I have some things to think through. Since my engagement broke up, I've had a lot of unanswered questions."

She took a deep purifying breath, steadying herself against the avalanches of pain tumbling over her. It was still incomprehensible how she'd been so easily and thoroughly deceived. But she resolutely lifted her auburn-crowned head to face her friends.

"I've learned a lesson—the hard way." Her wry smile belied the emotion twisting within her. "What a man believes is what counts. No more smooth-talkin' city dudes for me. Just straightshooters like Arne, here." She touched the older man's arm in fond camaraderie. "But enough serious conversation!" She went on, pushing herself away from the table. "I think I'll go up to the chateau for a look around." Troubled thoughts about the previous night ran through her mind, but Arne dispersed them with a pat on the shoulder and the command legendary in Medora.

" 'Hasten forward quickly there.' "

She grinned broadly as he gave her a playful wink, tipped an imaginary bowler hat, and sauntered from the cafe with Jean at his side. Katelyn could imagine the originator of those infamous words, a young Harvard-educated dandy trying to make an impression on the rough-hewn cowboys of the Badlands by spewing out the fateful and imperious command to hurry. Theodore Roosevelt no doubt heard his words over and over during the years he spent in the Badlands, for his command became a frontier slogan, used primarily in saloons to prod dawdling innkeepers to faster service.

Cheered, she jogged back to her car at the house. This time she would have a faster route of escape should she meet any strangers on the bluffs by the chateau.

She drove the mile to the ridge on the river bank opposite the town. The massive house rested like a gray fortress commanding a panoramic view of the Little Missouri and all that de Mores once owned.

Suspended anew in the web of romance and intrigue surrounding de Mores, Katelyn strolled toward the front door, her active imagination re-creating the lives of the marquis and his marquise. So preoccupied was she with her whimsy, she did not perceive the musky, masculine scent on the breeze or the long, dark shadow that had fallen over the doorway she was about to enter. Not until her arm had brushed his black shirt sleeve did she realize she had nearly stumbled over her nemesis of the night before.

"You've got to be more careful where you're walking," the rich voice chided mildly, the hint of a smile somewhere behind the gently scolding words. He grasped her by the arms and steered her to a clearer path.

Sputtering and indignant, Katelyn found herself face to face with the one person in Medora she had hoped never to see again.

"Please let go of me!" She struggled vainly to free herself from his intimate and distressing grip. She was suddenly aware of the brisk cologne and the mat of curly dark hair that peeked from beneath his open shirt at her eye level.

Accommodating her wishes, he dropped his hands to his sides and released her. Still squirming from his grasp, however, she lost her balance and sprawled backward, arms flailing wildly for the door facing. She landed hard on the bruise of the night before, blanched in pain, and emitted a pitiful moan.

Cheerfully unsympathetic and with a playful twinkling in his dark eyes, her tormentor began to chuckle. Then his shoulders shook with laughter. He kept on laughing as he extended a helping hand to the prone Katelyn.

"Sorry, ah–ha, I can't help it.... You're just an accident waiting to…happen. Who are you anyway?"

"Who am *I*? Who are you? What right have you to be up here, scaring people, causing them to fall…?" Her tirade ended in a breathy sputter as the absurdity of the situation struck her. She quelled the giggle that threatened.

"Now, don't be touchy. I have every right to be here, and as far as I know, you don't. We usually arrest trespassers at the chateau. This is your second offense in less than twenty-four hours. Persistent, aren't you?"

17

She felt a blush ignite her cheeks, but she responded gamely. "Well, I do have reason to be here. As I told you last night, I'll be working at the chateau this summer. In fact, I have my own key. Now what do you have to say to that?"

Observing her unconsciously rubbing her bruised hip as she spoke, he answered with an engaging smile. "You should take better care of that, madam. Seems to me you're pretty hard on your derriére. Come on, let's go have some coffee and decide what we're going to do about you."

Katelyn threw up her hands. Would this cowboy ever take her seriously? Then again, she'd taken more pratfalls in his presence than she cared to think about. Mustering the shreds of her dignity, she began hobbling down the hill.

After pausing to close and lock the door of the chateau, the cowboy caught up to her in a few strides and amiably matched his step to her tortoise-like gait. She gritted her teeth and kept walking, eyes straight ahead, unwilling to admire openly the dark-haired man beside her who so resembled the handsome marquis.

At the parking level, he paused and turned toward her, genuine concern flickering in his eyes. "Are you all right? Do you want me to drive?"

Unwillingly Katelyn reached for the hand he offered.

"Maybe so." Her hip was beginning to throb. Since it was his fault she'd tumbled again, driving to the cafe was the least he could do.

His touch, firm but gentle, sent shivers through her as he helped her into the car and she felt a jolt of surprise at her response. She'd begun to believe a man's touch would never affect her again.

"This must be what they call an economy car. You

18

can tell what they economized on—space." He grimaced as he bent his legs under the steering wheel.

"Your legs are too long."

"Well, I think I'll keep them this length and just travel the way I usually do."

"And how is that?" she inquired with saccharine sweetness. "By jackass?"

His laughter reverberated in the confines of the car. "Close. By horse, mostly. I'm running one of the trail rides."

Katelyn bolted upright. "Are you the one who bought the stable and trail rides from old Jake Pelton?"

"Luke Stanton, at your service. Trail guide, animal resource manager, temporary caretaker, and night watchman at the chateau. That's my excuse for being there. Now do you want to tell me a little more about yours?"

"Katelyn Ryan. My father is Ben Ryan, a ranger in Theodore Roosevelt National Park. I'm one of the tour guides at the chateau this summer. I just returned yesterday and I thought I'd look around and refresh my memory."

"You've got marquis fever, too, I suppose. Everyone around here seems to."

She quirked an eyebrow in his direction. "I'm surprised you aren't afflicted yourself since you so resemble his pictures." She studied the firm profile beside her. Luke Stanton could easily have posed for one of the de Mores portraits.

"Here we are," Luke remarked as they pulled up to the Rough Rider. "Still want that coffee?"

She shrugged, intrigued. "Why not?"

"All right. Let me help you out of this peanut of a car." He unfolded himself and strode around to the passenger side to extricate Katelyn. He set her upright,

19

his hands wedged under her arms. A twinge of alarm slithered through her at the cowboy's touch and she shivered slightly in the hot morning sun.

"You're just the people I wanted to see!" Arne was chugging toward them grinning in delight. "I'm glad to see you've met." He crossed his arms Buddha-fashion across his expansive girth. "Where did you run into each other?"

"At the chateau." Luke's answer was clipped, expressionless.

Katelyn looked at him from the corner of her eye. The cowboy stayed silent. Only a gleam in his eye and a grin tugging at the corner of his lip signaled that he hadn't forgotten her upside-down tumble on the hill.

Her eyes thanking Luke for his silence, she spoke to Arne. "We're going to have coffee. Care to join us?"

"Most definitely. Come on." Arne led the way into the cafe.

"I've gathered that Luke here is another expert on Medora history," Arne remarked as he scooted his bulk under the table. "I'd venture to say he knows as much about the region as you do, Katelyn."

She sat back in her chair, looking at the cowboy in a new light. "Then why did you ask me about having 'marquis fever,' Mr. Stanton? Seems as though you have a touch of it yourself."

"I'd rather live in the present than the past, Miss Ryan. And I don't like being compared to some long-dead local hero." A smile played across his features, "After all, I may have some heroic qualities of my own!"

She smiled. "Perhaps I *am* a bit obsessive about the Marquis de Mores, but he's what Medora is all about."

"Well," Luke interjected, "if you're going to spend the morning talking ancient history, I think I'll get to work. I have some horses that need tending."

He rose from his seat in one fluid motion, the backs of his calves pushing the caned chair from under his hips with a sharp, scraping sound. He dug deep into the pocket of his jeans and pulled out a five-dollar bill. Tossing it onto the table, he gave Katelyn an appealing wink. "When you're ready to talk about the present, come on out to the stables and I'll show you around." With that he sauntered into the street, broad shoulders rolling under the fabric of his shirt.

"He's a good-looking man, isn't he?" Arne commented.

Katelyn shot him a suspicious look. "Forget the matchmaking. I've had enough of men for a while, Arne. Anyway, looks aren't everything."

"Something—or someone—has taught you a hard lesson, hasn't he, kitten?"

"I thought I could tell the good men from the bad, but I've found I can't, Arne. So I've given them up entirely. It's far less painful than making another mistake. Luke Stanton could be the Marquis de Mores and I wouldn't be interested."

"But, kitten…"

She shook her flaming curls. "I don't trust men anymore. And there's not a man alive who's going to change my mind."

Arne raised an eyebrow. "We'll see about that. You might find Luke Stanton different from any other man you've known."

Shooting her friend a skeptical look, she rose from the table. "Never," she said emphatically. "Never!"

Chapter Two

Out in the dry noontime air, with tourists jostling her on all sides, Katelyn's racing thoughts turned back to Medora. Little had changed since her last visit home. The old cattle town's ambiance remained.

The original settlement across the river was a scraggly place called Little Missouri, made of the Pyramid Park Hotel and the buildings of the Badlands Cantonment which had protected railroad workers from the Indians. The hamlet's nickname, "Little Misery," eloquently characterized the place it had been.

Prostitutes had outnumbered more refined ladies, and gamblers, drifters, rustlers, con men, thieves, gunmen, and other human leeches occasionally populated the tiny Dakota town. Illustrious eastern sportsmen traveled West to hunt there, thus filling the Pyramid Park Hotel on a regular basis.

Little Misery was one of the toughest little towns on the Northern Pacific railroad line. Arguments were settled with a gun in the tiny isolated settlement. From what Katelyn had heard and read, there had been only twenty-four permanent residents. But the population fluctuated greatly, embracing outlaws and renegades who did not want their whereabouts known. Into this questionable community came the swashbuckling French nobleman, the Marquis de Mores.

Katelyn wished whimsically that such notable businesses as "Big-Mouthed Bob's Bug-Juice Dispensary" still existed. Feeling aimless and vaguely sad, she kicked at a clump of sagebrush on the roadside. Randy Baker was to blame for this....

Charming, magnetic, dishonest Randy. Even her parents did not know the full truth yet. She shuddered, wondering how to explain to her parents that her former fiancé was in jail.

"Don't blame yourself, Miss Ryan. Baker is a troubled man," the kindly police officer had said, sympathizing with the trembling young woman huddled in a wooden chair by his desk. "Don't blame yourself. I'd advise you to start over, pull your life back together ...somehow."

She had known at once where to come to begin again. The Badlands...home.

Suddenly purposeful, she strode to her car, ignoring the painful ache of her bruised hip.

"Katelyn, where are you going?"

She whirled to face her father, trim and polished in his ranger's uniform.

"Hi, Daddy. Just to the lookout over the park. I didn't stop yesterday when I passed it. I was too anxious to see you and Mom."

He smiled. "Then that's the first! I've never been able to drive by that jog in the road without your begging me to stop. You don't ever tire of that view, do you?"

"I haven't in twenty-six years."

"Run along then. Stare at the hills all you want. You aren't the only one who thinks they're beautiful."

She flashed a grateful smile and slid into the car. The

short walk had helped. Her leg wasn't so stiff. Eagerly she pulled into the street and headed for the overlook.

Vans and campers already lined the parking area, and families were posing at the massive stone marker that welcomed visitors to Theodore Roosevelt National Park. She ignored them all and aimed for the spot that provided a panoramic view of her beloved Badlands. Standing at the edge of the cliff, she drank in the rugged beauty of her home.

The unchanging yet forever changing Badlands greeted her. A shocking, alien land rising up from the gently rolling plains of North Dakota, the Badlands were a startling contrast to the majestic flatness to both east and west. Suddenly, out of lush green prairie, chains of towering buttes rose, silhouetted against an azure sky.

Brigadier General Alfred Sully had once described the Badlands as "hell with the fires out." Yet Katelyn was bewitched by the ever-changing beauty and haunting grandeur of the lonesome disdainful hills. The rolling grassland, sculpted buttes, carved-out canyons, and bluffs arranged in nature's most perfect maze welcomed her home.

Surely *here* things were as they seemed. Thoughts of Randy were as treacherous as strands of tall grass in the dry creek beds that harbored bottomless pools of ooze and slime. Quicksand—drawing the unsuspecting into a suffocating, engulfing trap.

She sighed deeply, her hands gripping the guardrail. She'd come home emotionally battered and scarred, hoping to heal and regain the strength to continue.

She glanced over her shoulder at the beaming visage of Teddy Roosevelt on the park sign. He had come here in 1884 after the double tragedy of the untimely deaths of his wife and mother. The rigors of life in the

Badlands had kept him sane. She sought some source of strength as well.

She shook herself mentally and smiled. The Badlands always made her feel this way, happy and sad, old and young, weak and strong. In a land of contradictions, it seemed fitting to feel full of contradictions herself.

As she gazed toward the horizon, she remembered the words Roosevelt himself had written about the Badlands, "When one is in the Badlands he feels as if they somehow *look* just exactly as Poe's tales and poems *sound*." In the days after Randy's bleak revelation, when she found herself searching out an old and nearly forgotten book of Edgar Allan Poe's poetry, she had known it was time to go home.

She turned from the panoramic view and strolled to her car. A healthy, hungry feeling was beginning to gnaw at her insides; her appetite was finally returning.

Revving the engine, she slipped the car into gear. An impulsive thought niggled at her as she passed the trail ride signs on the outskirts of town. Perhaps a friendly visit to Mr. Marquis-look-alike Stanton wouldn't be such a bad idea after all. Jake Pelton had taught her to ride, and she'd spent a good share of her childhood under his roof hearing him spin yarns. Curiosity compelled her to see if Luke had changed old Jake's home.

Impetuously, she pulled onto the ragged dirt road leading to the stables. The claptrap conglomeration of lean-tos and pole barns seemed hardly able to stand by themselves, but a new log cabin nestled in the embrace of the hill, its rough-hewn logs still unweathered by rain and sun.

No cars dotted the parking lot, and Katelyn approached the buildings stealthily, a bit unsure of her welcome. Jake's old dog Gus lay sleeping in the sun, and he lazily opened one eye. She could hear the thump-thump-thump of his tail on the hard-packed ground as she passed.

"Hello. So you decided to come."

She gasped involuntarily as the voice greeted her from the shadows of the tack room. "Luke?"

"Come on in. I'm fixing a saddle."

She felt her way into the dim recess, blinking rapidly as she adjusted to the shadows. She inhaled deeply, savoring the familiar smells of polished leather and horses. "It smells just the same!"

A low chuckle came from the far corner. "You really *are* a country girl, aren't you? Some of the tourists through here don't seem to enjoy the aroma at all."

When her eyes had adapted to the dimness, she could see Luke bending over a saddle. A battered straw cowboy hat sat far back on his head. Tight new denims swathed his legs, and in place of the black shirt was a clear red Western shirt, sleeves sawed off at the shoulders to reveal thick, smooth arms bathed in a golden tan. As he turned to her, a filtered beam of light caught the silver of his belt buckle.

"Want a tour?"

Startled from her visual feast, Katelyn stumbled a bit before answering. "Sure. Why not? I mean, that's what I came for, isn't it?"

"Is it?" Luke had a disconcerting way of asking questions. He reached his arm upward to scratch the head of a tiny kitten sleeping in the saddle mounted just over his head. Suddenly a wisp of fur grazed her ankle, and Katelyn realized the tack room was full of the tiny creatures.

"There were never any cats here when Jake ran this place," she commented as she picked up the black and white mass purring at her feet.

"They made him sneeze. The cats were my first innovation. How do you like it?"

Her voice came back muffled as she buried her nose in soft fur. "Just fine. How does Gus the mutt handle it?"

"He's too old to care. The only time he complains is when one falls asleep on his nose."

Katelyn chuckled. "Well, let's see what else has been going on." She lowered the kitten to a pile of hay near the door and followed Luke into the sunlight.

"Most everything is the same. I've added new horses, and next year I'll build a new barn if I can afford it."

He began to work his way through the horses with Katelyn following closely at his heels. He spoke to each one, calling them by name, patting their rumps fondly.

"I see you've built a new house."

"Jake was a fine man but a terrible housekeeper. I finally set a match to the shack after spending a week trying to fix it up. Built the cabin myself. Want to see it?"

Katelyn nodded eagerly, surprising herself.

They stepped over Gus, who had sunk into a nearly comatose state, and into the cabin. It was fragrant with new wood and leather. Empty except for a single cot and heap of stone in the middle of the floor, it looked rough and uninviting.

"You live *here*?" Her voice pitched upward in amazement.

"I'm not done yet, you know. Just wait. I'm working on the fireplace now. Give me a couple of weeks to finish."

"But where do you cook and, well, never mind."

"Shower? Listen, lady, I'm not *that* primitive." He

27

nodded to doors on the far side of the room. "Bathroom's on the left, kitchen on the right. All plumbed and wired with every modern convenience. I just didn't want all the gadgets to distract from the main room, so I hid them. Go look if you don't believe me."

Giving him an incredulous glance, she opened one of the doors. Before her was a tiny galley kitchen complete with refrigerator and microwave oven.

"Amazing! You'd never even know it was there!" She pulled the door shut and turned toward the other one. At once she giggled from behind the second door. "Luke Stanton! Whatever made you do this?"

He ambled to the door and twisted his head around the corner. Katelyn stood in the middle of a room twice the size of the kitchen. She tapped one foot on a sunken whirlpool and rested her hand across a mirrored vanity.

"Some rugged life you lead. Jake Pelton would do flip-flops in his grave if he knew his old home now has cats and a sunken bathtub."

Luke chuckled. "I ride all day, every day—unless, of course, I'm moving hay or roping. I break a few horses on the side and chase critters through the park for the animal resource management people. The only luxury I want is a hot soak at the end of the day. That's not so frivolous, is it?"

"You forgot to mention the winters out here. You could use it to thaw out as well."

"Good point. When twenty below zero is the day's high, it should come in handy."

"But are you ever going to decorate?" she queried, moving again into the greatroom and kicking at the pile of stone for the fireplace.

"Right after the fireplace is in. I'll have you back for a showing—if you're still around."

"What do you mean, if I'm still here? Where else would I be?

"Back where you came from."

"I came from here, Luke. Remember?"

"You grew up here. People change in the city. Maybe there won't be enough for you here anymore."

Her laugh was scornful. "There was too much of a lot of things for me in the city, Luke—lies, dishonesty, pain…men. But I don't want to get into that. Medora is going to be just fine for me."

Luke raised a questioning eyebrow, but he did not pursue the enigmatic statement. Silently he led her back into the sunlight and toward the car.

Grateful for his lack of curiosity, Katelyn bestowed one of her most charming smiles on the puzzling Luke. "I'd better be going now. My stomach's beginning to growl. All I've had this morning is more than my share of coffee."

Luke's hand rested on her car door, preventing her from closing it. "You have plans for lunch, I suppose?"

"Not really. Maybe I'll stop at home and see what's in the cupboard. I'm a bit at loose ends yet. Once I begin working at the chateau, I'll get organized."

"I'm taking the Jeep into the park to see if I can spot some mule deer. Want to pack a lunch and come with me?"

Astounded that he had asked and more astonished still that she wanted to go, Katelyn stammered an acceptance. "I suppose I could. I mean—they aren't expecting me home."

"Are you fussy?"

"No, I don't think so. What did you have in mind?"

"Come on." He led the way back to the kitchen and tossed open the refrigerator door. He stood, legs wide apart, hands on hips, studying the contents. Soon he

29

began pulling items from the shelves. "Smoked turkey. Beef jerky. Potatoes. Apples. Butter. Marshmallows. Coke." From the cabinet he took salt and pepper and foil.

Katelyn's eyes widened as he tossed the conglomeration into a cardboard box with paper plates and silverware.

"There. Let's go." He picked up the box and started for the door.

"Luke," she interrupted hesitantly, hating to criticize the odd combination, "those potatoes you put in the box are raw."

He turned back to her, his arms still folded around the groceries. A smile played at his lips. "I know."

Her hunger rapidly abating, she followed him to a rugged little Jeep replete with ropes, guns, and equipment she didn't recognize. Luke tossed the dubious grocery box in back and swung into the seat. Katelyn scrambled to follow, and in minutes they were jouncing their way toward the park entrance.

"Hi, Luke! Working or playing today?" the guard at the entrance inquired, studying Katelyn openly with a gleam of frank envy in her eyes.

"A little of both. I'm looking for some mule deer and whitetails. I'd like to get a head count if I can. And I need to find a hot spot for a picnic."

"Just don't tell the world what you're up to!" she responded and waved him through.

Things were getting more and more curious, Katelyn thought as they wound their way upward into the park. Soon, however, she forgot about Luke and his lunch as she gazed over the Badlands.

Her eyes roamed hungrily across the postcard-perfect panorama, savoring the land of startling contradictions. Hills and buttes, valleys and canyons lay side by side, some lush and verdant at the wooded river bottom and some barren and parched like the scarred ridges rising above them. The land simultaneously repelled and enticed her with its vastness, lonely grandeur, and terrifying silence.

Luke veered into an overlook, allowing her to gaze at the land before her. Tearing her eyes away from the view, she met his understanding gaze.

"It is spectacular, isn't it?"

"One of a kind. So many times, I've wished I were surrounded by hills instead of glass and steel. I'm glad I'm home."

"But will that last, Katelyn?" Luke asked, an odd tone in his voice.

"Why shouldn't it?"

"Once you begin to run away from something, it seems you always have to keep running."

A dart of pain shimmered in her chest. Luke had aptly read the emotions she'd struggled to hide. "What makes you think I'm running away from something, Luke?"

"I don't think it's a 'something,' Katelyn. I think it's a 'who.' And you're running scared."

He listened too well and saw too much. But there was no reason for him ever to know about Randy. She'd never allow herself close enough to be hurt by a man again. A cold, hard light glittered in her eyes.

Seeing the icy warning, Luke shifted the Jeep into gear and pulled into the roadway. "We'd better get to our picnic spot or it's going to be supper we're eating."

Katelyn slumped limply against the seat. Luke Stanton seemed able to come dangerously close to the chinks in her armor. She'd have to reinforce her defenses.

"Well, here we are." He flipped off the ignition and

31

jumped from the vehicle. He pulled a shovel from the Jeep and tucked the questionable groceries under one arm. Katelyn jogged to keep up with him as he headed for a barren patch of earth.

"Here, wrap foil around these potatoes, and we'll toss 'em in."

"Toss them in what? Did you bring an oven?"

"No, but nature provided one. There's a coal vein burning near the surface here. I'll dig a hole in the ground and we'll toss them in and cover them with dirt. The potatoes will bake while we go look for my deer."

"I've read about people doing this! I didn't think it could be done here anymore. Isn't the coal burning too far below the surface now?"

"This is the only spot I know of where it still works, and I wouldn't publicize it. Next thing you know a tourist would get himself cooked trying to roast a marshmallow. Your father is the one who showed me how."

"Daddy? Do you know Daddy?"

"Medora is hardly big enough for us to be strangers, Katelyn. We've worked together several times. Nice fellow. Come on. I've got deer to count."

The minutes passed quickly as they scanned the jagged hills. The age-wrinkled walls of the buttes gleamed with nature's colors, the drab yellow and gray of clay, black and purple lines of coal, and streaks of red scoria, burnt clay. Green pines and cedars dotted the sloping landscape, and Katelyn looked down for a moment at her feet nestled in silvery sage.

Soon she felt Luke's breath waft against her cheek. "Look at the white-tailed deer. Can you see them? Be quiet and they may come closer."

As the shy creatures edged toward the immobile

couple on the hillside, Katelyn found herself worrying that the thudding of her heart would scare them away. Luke had grabbed her elbow in his excitement, and his fingers dug into the soft hollows of her arm. His breath came in ragged rhythm as he watched the large herd come nearer.

Katelyn found dormant emotions igniting. Since Randy's deceit, Luke was the first man who had touched her and not caused her to cringe. With the rebirth of those sensations, though, came new fear. Luke might hurt her just as Randy had. Until he could prove he was different, Luke Stanton would have to be resisted like all the others. She stiffened against the firm, warm pressure of his body.

"Think our potatoes are ready?"

The question jarred her back to the present. The animals rambled away, and Luke's arm wandered across her shoulders. Shrugging off his embrace more easily than her thoughts, she turned to face him.

"What are we waiting for? Let's go find out!"

"Luke, this is absolutely wonderful!" Katelyn licked buttery fingers as she spoke.

Luke grinned and tugged some more at the jerky between his teeth. "I know. You just didn't trust me."

"You *are* the first man I've known who wanted to take raw potatoes on a picnic."

"I wouldn't let you down, Katelyn."

She shot him a questioning look, but he only smiled and stretched his long legs across the sparse grass and leaned more heavily on the rock that supported him. His hat shaded his eyes, and he looked as much a part of the scenery as the sand hill crane that circled lazily overhead.

Katelyn curled her knees to her chest and watched

33

him. Finally one eye opened under the hat, and a lazy voice drawled. "Whatcha lookin' at?"

"You."

"Whatcha thinkin' about?"

"You."

"What about me?"

"I'm just imagining you riding in these hills, chasing whatever it is you like to chase."

The hat moved as he chuckled. "Cattle, mostly. I work roundups when I can."

"You and Teddy Roosevelt."

Luke crossed his legs and stretched out farther in the sage. "Hardly. He was a glutton for punishment. I read he once spent forty hours in the saddle and wore out four horses doing it. Now me," and he tilted the hat backward so Katelyn could see his expression, "I like to come home and crawl into that nice big tub after a long day."

She laughed at the smile in his eyes. "You're the oddest cowboy I've ever met, that's for sure." She settled back for a moment then sat bolt upright, frozen. "Luke! What was that?"

"What was what?" He'd pulled the hat back into place over his eyes.

"I think I heard a rattlesnake."

"I didn't hear anything."

"Well I did. What should I do?"

"Don't scare it."

"*Scare* it? What do you think it's doing to me? There! There it is again!" She edged closer to the lounging cowboy.

"That's not a rattler, Katelyn. It's locusts."

"Are you sure?" She insisted, looking suspiciously at the spot where the noise originated. She worked her way toward Luke until her knee grazed the sole of his

34

boot and her hand rested close to his elbow.

"Yup." With one lazy motion he sat up and gazed at the point in question. Their shoulders brushed together, and Katelyn found her face only inches from the rim of his hat. He turned toward her and smiled. "I just love locusts."

"What? Why?"

"They got you moved over here, next to me, didn't they? Come on, I'll share my backrest."

She leaned against the sun-warmed stone, soaking up the sizzling rays, one shoulder nestled beneath Luke's arm.

Warm, full, and sleepy, she knew she should be enjoying the lazy siesta. Instead, she was battling a clenching ache in her midsection. The golden arm draped around her only conjured up images of Randy Baker and the many times he'd held her.

Nothing was as it seemed. Luke—the Marquis de Mores—Teddy Roosevelt—Randy...this day had blended them all together in a confusing jumble. Past and present melded in the hot sun, and a tear dripped silently down her cheek.

A feather-light touch wiped the tear away. Luke's eyes searched her face for answers to unasked questions. The single tear glistened on his fingertip and he wiped it dry on the seam of his jeans. Softly he spoke. "Don't run away any more, Katelyn—from whatever it is that's haunting you. Maybe I could help."

She scrambled upward. "How could you help? You're part of the problem. All men are. Take me home, Luke. Now."

In silence they drove the winding highway toward Medora.

Chapter Three

Blast that Luke Stanton!

Katelyn slammed kettles and a blackened cast-iron skillet about her mother's tranquil kitchen, feeling very much like a minor tempest in this teapot of a house. The hot sun seeped through every crack and cranny, wrapping her in warm, seductive fingers. And Luke was as insinuating as the sun, worming his way into her emotions—reawakening feelings she believed had been left behind.

With a determined tilt to her chin, she vowed to fortify her defenses against the charming Luke. In one idyllic day in the Badlands he'd almost lulled her into complacency. Men were full of chicanery and dark ways. Randy had taught her that.

"What's all the noise out here?" Ben Ryan peered around the door frame, his brow furrowed in concern. "A localized earthquake, perhaps? Centered on top of the kitchen counter?"

"Sorry, Daddy, I just got carried away." Katelyn grinned sheepishly at her father as he polished his balding head with the palm of his hand. "I was thinking of something else, and the pans just started to clatter."

"And clang, bang, and crash Katie, me darlin', for your birthday I'll buy you cymbals."

Her eyes brightened at the teasing Irish lilt her father feigned. He'd been no closer to Ireland than the nearest encyclopedia, but his love for the country filled their shelves with history books and the music of his parents' former homeland. His bonny red-haired daughter was Ben's crowning glory, and the pride he felt for her shone in his eyes.

But those admiring eyes clouded, and Katelyn steeled herself for what was forthcoming.

"All that noise isn't like you, Katelyn. You're usually not given to slamming my lunch about. Do you want to talk about it?"

Suddenly and fervently Katelyn wished her mother hadn't driven into Dickinson to shop. Her presence always protected Katelyn from her father's probing questions.

"Nothing, Daddy. Really." She hastily slid the grilled cheese sandwiches onto a serving platter and pushed it toward her father. Turning her back on his appraising eyes, she spooned hot tapioca pudding into custard cups. She'd cooked her father's favorites. Perhaps lunch would make him forget about the inquisition.

But the look on his face told her otherwise when she pulled up a chair across from him at the table. Listlessly, she slipped a sandwich onto her plate, waiting.

"Well?" He laid his fork across his plate. "What happened?"

"Between Randy and me, you mean?"

"That's as good a place to start as any." Ben settled into the chair.

She sighed and reached for the coffeepot and set it between them. It was going to be a long lunch hour. She gave her father the abbreviated version of her breakup with Randy, the one she'd rehearsed all the way across Minnesota and North Dakota.

"So you say he didn't love you, Katelyn? I find that hard to believe."

"You would, Daddy. You've loved me too long to know how to do anything else." Katelyn smiled gently. "But I didn't know Randy as well as I thought I did. He did some...things.... I made a mistake, that's all. I never should have trusted a man with such a smooth, suave, polished line. I was swept off my feet. But I'm going to be more careful from now on." Her voice sharpened more than she had intended.

"And is that why you came home from the stables last night in such a foul mood?"

Katelyn's head jerked up with a start. "How did you know I was at the stables?"

"You're in Medora, now, my dear." Ben chuckled. "Everyone knows everything. The ranger at the park entrance saw you and Luke take his Jeep into the park. It only follows that when you came home, it was from the stables."

She suppressed a bubbling laugh. She had forgotten the joys and trials of small-town life. Every resident knew every other. In Chicago, she'd never met her neighbors. Here, the entire city was both neighbor and friend.

"Luke and I had a very nice day, Dad. Nothing more."

"A nice day, you say? Since when does a nice day make you mope around the house all evening? And since when does a nice day make you slam around the kitchen with swipes that would crack cast iron? If Luke said or did something that hurt you..." His eyes darkened and he clenched his fork in a knuckle-whitening grip.

"Oh, no, Daddy! Nothing like that! Luke was a perfect gentleman. It was a beautiful day. Only…"

"Only what, Katelyn?"

"It made me think of Randy. We used to have beautiful days together, too. He'd tell me how much he loved me. We'd talk about the day we would be married and have a house…and children. I believed him! And none of it was true! Now he's…" She chomped down hard on her inner lip. She'd almost let it slip—that Randy was in jail.

"Now he's what, Katelyn?" Ben had seen the obvious paling of her features and the tense set of her jaw.

"Now he's gone. Forever. And I'm never going to let myself get caught in a situation like that again." The stubborn thrust of her jaw punctuated her resolve.

"You're never going to fall in love again? Darlin', that doesn't sound promising to a man who wants grandchildren!"

"Well, at least not for a long, long time."

"And this is where Luke Stanton comes in," Ben crowed, startling Katelyn from her pensiveness.

"And just what do you mean by that?"

"All those feelings you want to ignore, all those men you want to hate. Katie, me darlin', I'll wager that our handsome Luke reminded you how hard it was going to be to keep that promise to yourself!" A wide smile sliced across Ben's features.

Katelyn had the grace to hang her head. Her father's speculative arrow had hit the bull's eye. His delighted laughter wrapped its arms about her.

"Dad…" she began.

"No, Katie, me darlin', don't say a word! *I* want to say something first. Don't toss this Randy fellow and Luke into the same bag. I'd bet any amount they're no more alike than night and day. Don't run away from

Luke Stanton this summer, Katelyn. He's solid, strong. Ask him what's important to him. You might be surprised."

Surprised. That's what she'd been with Randy. Surprised at his infidelity, at the news he was an embezzler. Lately all the surprises in her life had been painful ones.

"I'm going by the stables on my way back to work. Luke has a new colt he wants me to see. Born only last night. Interested in coming along?" Ben pushed his empty plate away and tipped backward in the dinette chair, grinding the back legs deep into the soft linoleum floor. Katelyn winced, knowing what her mother would say, but daughter and father had been cohorts too long for her to take on her mother's disciplinary role now.

"I don't think so, Dad. Maybe later."

"Later it won't be a brand new baby. They're incredible little creatures. You've never been able to pass up an opportunity like this before."

She had to admit to her fondness for horses. Fortunately for her, Jake Pelton had had the patience of Job, tolerating her continual presence and unending stream of questions at his stable. She'd learned a great deal from the wizened old man—and had never been able to resist stroking a new colt.

"Oh, all right. But don't go smirking and being coy around Luke Stanton. I meant what I said, Dad. I'm through with men for a while. I'm impervious to Cupid's arrows, so leave them in their quiver!"

As they neared the barns, Katelyn began to chastise herself for weakening. Marching into the stables with her father was hardly the best way to distance herself from Luke. She feared her attraction to him most of all.

But Luke was oblivious to her distress and intent on

the saddle he was repairing, barely glancing up as they walked into the tack room.

"Hi." A lank piece of straw angled from the corner of his mouth. He pushed his battered hat back with the heel of one grimy hand.

"Things falling apart?" Ben inquired, leaning low over the saddle to see Luke's handiwork.

"Just about everything. Poor Jake mended some of this stuff so many times there isn't any original left. I'm not as adept as he was at spinning gold from straw. I'm going to order more new saddles at the beginning of the month." With a frustrated jab at the offending pillion, Luke stood.

Katelyn watched him unwind from his perch like a smooth liquid stream. He was built like an inverted triangle, wide and solid at the shoulders, narrowing to trim, sinewy hips. Even in the dusky light of the tack room, his skin had the glow of warmed honey. Unaccountably, Katelyn thought of Luke in terms of tastes and smells—golden honey, newly cut hay, fragrant breezes, heady musk—earthy, natural, compelling.

Obviously unaware of the reactions he was inspiring, he swung one long leg over the top of the battered saddle and cocked his head toward the long, low barn. "Want to see my new baby?"

"That's what we came for, my boy," Ben rejoined. "I do believe Katelyn would have stayed home if there were any other drawing card, but a new colt will bring her here any time of the day or night!"

Katelyn would have loved to stuff her fist into her father's mouth, but his comment was already out. She could feel Luke's eyes studying her speculatively as he commented, "I'll have to remember that."

Luke led them toward the barn and the soft dirt of the corral shifted under their feet. As they sidestepped

41

suspicious piles, Katelyn wished she'd worn her work boots. But the colt was worth it. All legs and head, she stood near her mother. Already, the spindly limbs were steadying, struggling to leave babyhood behind. The colt gleamed a soft, smooth red.

"Like burnished copper!" Katelyn breathed, unaware she'd spoken aloud.

Luke glanced back over his shoulder and nodded in delight. "I thought so, too. In fact, I almost decided to name her Copper Penny. She looks like one, all shiny and bright."

"And you didn't? That's a beautiful name for a colt!" Katelyn moved forward and buried her fingers in the babe's neck, crooning and scratching. Her father was being nudged out of hearing by curious horses reaching over the stall for sugar cubes in his pockets.

"I thought of a better one," Luke commented tersely.

She glanced up, surprised. "What could be better than Copper Penny?"

"What do you think of Irish Lass? I was thinking of another redhead I know."

A burning blush set her neck and cheeks on fire. When she was truly embarrassed—or flattered—she blushed all over. Even her toes felt pink and glowing under their grubby cover of shoes and barn dirt.

"It's...nice."

"I'm glad you like it." He shifted his weight from one foot to the other and swept the battered hat from his head, exposing his dark cap of hair to the sunlight. If Katelyn was burnished copper, he was obsidian— dark and smooth, glistening with natural luster.

Again she was struck by his resemblance to the Marquis de Mores. Slim, with a suggestion of wiry power and a cloak of natural, easy elegance and grace even in

42

humble work clothes, both he and those ancient photos of de Mores could stir the female heart.

He spread his hands wide and rubbed the palms on the faded denim of his jeans. His denim workshirt was nearly white with washings. Only the bandana at his neck held a hint of newness. Suddenly she realized he was waiting for her to speak.

"Thank you, Luke. Irish Lass is a lovely name for this colt. We redheads have to stick together, you know. May I come and visit her again?" She found her lips saying the very thing her mind was warning against.

"That was my idea."

How straightforward he was! He played none of the coy flirting games to which she had become so accustomed. Seeds of delight and distress mingled in her consciousness. She couldn't let his candor disarm her. She was not ready to trust. Not yet.

"There you go again."

"What?" Katelyn's head shot up at Luke's words.

"You drifted off into that never-never land you were in the other day in the park. First you had that look on your face. Then you cried." Steadying himself with his elbow on the top board of the stall, Luke balanced his weight on one foot and angled the other in front of his leg, the toe of his boot buried in the dirt. He was studying her with that disconcerting look that pierced her like a saber.

Apprehension bolted through her like jagged lightning in the night sky, and she skittered away from his eyes. His perceptiveness frightened her. She did not want to be so readily understood. It made her too vulnerable, too easily hurt again.

"Katelyn, I have to get back to work. Do you want a ride home, or can you find your own way?" She had nearly forgotten her father's presence.

Glad to escape, she responded, "You can give me a ride, Dad. I'm sure Luke has plenty to do without any more city slickers under foot."

Luke chuckled. "I make my living showing city slickers the park, Katelyn. Don't say anything negative about my source of bread and butter. I do have a big group coming in pretty soon. Some convention is meeting out here, and they all want horses. But," and he paused theatrically, casting Katelyn a silent message, "I wouldn't mind company for a ride just before sunset. The hills are beautiful then."

Katelyn could hear her father swallow a chuckle. Luke had done it again. Tempting her with the most delectable of enticements—the Badlands at sunset. He had an uncanny sense of her weaknesses and strengths. Randy had *never* deduced her true emotions. Luke read them as if they were written on her sleeve.

"Well, I don't know, Luke. I'm not sure it's such a good idea...."

"I'll be waiting for you, Katelyn. The horses will be saddled. Come. Please?"

"Come on, Katelyn. I don't have time for you to hem and haw. If you decide not to go, you can tell the man later. I have to get back to work." She felt herself being propelled toward her father's vehicle, his strong hand steering her by the elbow. Luke did not follow them to the Jeep, and her last view was of the dark head bent low over the colt, long fingers gently kneading the baby's neck.

She ground her teeth on her index finger in dismay.

"What's the problem, Katelyn?" Ben asked, looking at her askance.

"Why would I want to take a ride with him at sunset? Why didn't I just say no?"

44

"Because you wanted to go, most likely. It's gorgeous out there at sunset—like watching God direct a play. The set changes with every movement of the sun, unfolding more colors. Those ugly, ravaged hills are the players, and they come alive on that stage at sunset, the silent voices of the past...."

"Daddy! That's simply beautiful!" Katelyn gasped, amazed at her father's impassioned and articulate description. She'd never heard him speak of God before—not with reverence, anyway.

He snorted softly, embarrassed. "I'm sorry, Katelyn. All I meant to tell you was to go with Luke. You'll enjoy it."

"Oh, I'm so confused! I came here swearing off men forever, and now I'm considering going out with one tonight!"

"A horseback ride is hardly a proposal of marriage, Katelyn. Good grief! Go riding with Luke! That's an order!" He paused in front of the house, and she stepped out onto the hard-packed street. Thoughtfully, she waved him away, still standing in the roadway long after his Jeep had disappeared from sight.

Hardly a proposal of marriage.

The memories came flooding back. Randy's face wheeled before her, blocking out the dusty street and the ragtag mop of weeds and grass in the ditch to her left. His blandly handsome features and smooth golden hair replaced the struggling flower beds her mother so diligently tended. She was in Chicago again.

Genteel, diffident, deferential Randy. A slick, social-climbing con man. How easily she'd fallen in love. How quickly she'd regretted it.

They had met at the YMCA where she worked.

"It's nice to meet you, Miss Ryan. My name is Randy Baker." He'd extended a sturdy, well-groomed hand

45

and shaken hers with firmness.

"And you, Mr. Baker. What can I do for you?"

"My company will be installing the new equipment in the south gymnasium. I'm to supervise the work. Just bear with me, Miss Ryan, and be kind when our noise disturbs your concentration."

New in the city and eager for a friendly face, Katelyn had fallen hook, line, and sinker for the handsome young man.

Snapping back to the present with the jolt of a released rubber band, she turned toward the house. The only thing to be gained in thinking of the past was the desire to bolster her reserve for the future.

But as the sun gradually dipped lower in the western sky, she found herself pulling on riding boots, perching a hat atop her riot of red curls, and walking hesitantly, puppetlike, toward the stables. Jerkily, she progressed down the street, careening forward eagerly for a moment, then pulling to a halt to ponder what she was about to do. The sun was low and flaming in the west as she made her way to Luke's front porch.

"Hi." He was leaning against the porch rail, silhouetted in the blaze of the sun. Captured by the disembodied voice, she put a cupped hand to her forehead to find his features in the brightness. He was in less-faded denims, and the damp wave on his forehead hinted at time spent in the big sunken tub in the cabin. As she neared she could smell the sweet tang of fresh soap.

"Hi, yourself." The staccato thump-thump-thump of Gus's tail beat on the toe of her boot.

"Hi, sweet fellow. Did you think I'd forget to say hello to you?" She scratched behind the limp ears and was rewarded with a redoubled thumping of his tail. Curious and jealous, a battalion of kittens descended on Katelyn's hand and Gus's head. He sneezed once, scattering the troops, and began a personal appeal for Katelyn's attentions.

"You have some new friends," Luke chuckled, picking up a gray and white fur ball and stroking it under the chin.

"So it seems." She kept her head bent and continued to stroke Gus's ears.

"I hope I'm included in that number."

She sat back on her heels and looked up into his face. "I think so."

"Let me know when you're sure." The somber look never left him as he spoke, and he extended a hand to Katelyn.

Rising gracefully, she dusted away imaginary soil. "Let's go on that ride you promised me."

Nodding, he led her to the stables where two horses were already saddled.

"Take your pick, Katelyn. They're my two best horses."

"Which one is less spirited? It's been a long time since I've been in the saddle. Maybe we should ride a bit before you decide to take me up and down the sides of buttes."

He chuckled. "These horses don't want to fall into the ravines any more than you do, Katelyn. They know where to go. Midnight and Wildfire could travel these trails in their sleep. In fact, I think sometimes they do. Poor things only wake up when some terrified tourist lets go of the saddle horn long enough to jerk on their manes."

She ran her hand deftly over the horse's flank, indicating more familiarity with the animals than she admitted. Then she swung into the saddle and settled herself against the creaking leather, her jeans sliding over the polished seat. Luke bent low over the stirrups, adjusting them to her long legs, and Katelyn fought the urge to run an idle finger through the black cap of his hair.

Satisfied, he swung into his own saddle and gave the horse its head.

Sunset in the Badlands was like nothing else in the world. The terraced hills of vermilion, purple, red, and blue came alive in a plethora of color.

Inexplicably, the twisted buttes created an odd sensation of terror and romance, hinting at gargoyles in a land with a history fraught with feuds and gunfire. Katelyn swayed easily in the saddle, the obedient horse beneath her following Luke's lead. In silent camaraderie they rode toward the fiery blaze of sunset.

Katelyn's mind strayed from the hills to the broad stretch of Luke's shoulders, and she edged her horse closer to his until they rode side by side. He turned his head slightly to acknowledge her presence and then returned his searching eyes to the grotesquely compelling landscape.

She smiled briefly. In his long, undemanding silences, Luke was more company than Randy had ever been. Randy had chattered of inconsequential things while Luke seemed only to speak when something mattered a great deal to him. She was struck with the peace, the tranquility that Luke wore as easily as his shirt and jeans.

They paused, looking over the Little Missouri, tracing its twisting path with their eyes. The river doubled back on itself until it reminded Katelyn of hairpin curves on a mountain road. The snaking flow of water had cut its valleys and ravines at angles to each other in an extraordinary natural maze.

"It's hard to believe there's two hundred fifty miles

of this, isn't it?" Luke's voice came out of the fading light. Katelyn jumped. She'd almost forgotten her silent partner could speak.

"I thought about it a lot as I came across Minnesota and North Dakota," she agreed. "First it's thick wooded land, and then prairies until you think they'll never end, that surely you can see the end of the world from where you are. Then suddenly that monotonous flatness ends and...."

" 'All geological hell breaks loose,' " Luke finished for her. "That's how Theodore Roosevelt described it."

"It must have been quite a place to come to then."

"Well, it was newer then. The lignite veins in the hills burned much nearer the surface. The Marquis de Mores probably could light a cigarette by reaching into a crevice. Now those veins have burned out or deep into the ground."

" 'Hell with the fires out,' " she murmured. General Sully's description seemed more apt than ever tonight as the shadows lengthened and the sun's flaming colors turned the hills strange and wild. A hushed unearthly expectancy hung over them. Katelyn shivered in her saddle. The misshapen shadows were both exhilarating and alarming.

"Let's get back to the stable before it's completely dark," Luke said. "Sometime soon we'll take a ride in the moonlight, but right now, I'd like some coffee."

Spying the barns, the horses broke into a trot. As the sun disappeared and darkness settled over the weirdly carved hills, the Badlands crouched silently, waiting for another day.

"Can you join me?" Luke inquired as they sauntered toward the cabin. Their shoulders rubbed as they walked, and though Katelyn's fingers itched to be held, Luke made no move to grasp the hand swinging at her side.

"I'd love to. Can I help?"

"No, thanks. Just sit on the porch and I'll be right out." He disappeared into the cabin, and a pale beam bled onto the wooden deck as he flicked on the kitchen light. Katelyn curled herself into the rocker and picked up a lapful of kittens.

"Here you are. Colombian. Hope you like it." He handed her a mug of the pungent, almost bitter coffee. The fragrant steam swirled into her nostrils as she sipped.

"Delicious!"

"Thanks. I order it and grind the beans myself. A luxury, but I like it."

"Like the bathtub?"

"Like the bathtub. Do you think I'm crazy?" He grinned a crooked, quirky grin.

"Not at all." *But I think I am!* She fought the attraction that was mushrooming within her for this surprising cowboy. What had happened to that vow of hers? Luke was more dangerous than she'd first believed.

She stood abruptly, the coffee splashing precariously near the rim of her cup. "I have to go, Luke. My parents will be wondering what happened to me." The lame excuse rang false even in her own ears, but Luke only nodded, set his own cup on the porch, and followed her down the steps.

He shoved his hands into his hip pockets and tilted back his head, his eyes burning black in the darkness as he stood quietly waiting.

She stepped toward him, drawn by her desire, wanting to explain her sudden inner panic, but as she moved his way, the toe of her boot grazed the inner arch of his own. Deftly Luke entwined his fingers in

50

her tumble of flaming hair and drew her to him. As she struggled to speak, his lips came down on hers, capturing the soft breath of her utterance.

It was a long, leisurely kiss tasting of sweet lips and bitter coffee. He rolled his head to one side and pressed light kisses against her cheek and ear, drawing from her a pleased little gasp.

Unconsciously she moved toward him until the thick, cold stone of his belt buckle grazed her midsection. Startled into reality, she stepped backward, away from this magnet of a man.

Excited yet afraid, she sought the cover of darkness to hide her ignited emotions and stumbled blindly toward home. Just as she thought she'd put a safe distance between herself and Luke, a disembodied voice came floating to her on the satiny night air.

"G'night, Katelyn."

She could see him standing on the porch, illuminated by the feeble interior lights. Tall, strong, masculine, Luke Stanton was part of this land—as beautiful, as exciting, as fearsome, and, to her, as dangerous.

As she made her way in the night, she scoured her brain for answers. She could no longer place him in the same category as other men—especially not Randy. What *was* it about Luke that made her feel so drawn to him, so sure of his incorruptible nature, his steadfastness?

Chapter Four

"You can't laze about the house all day, Katelyn. Your job begins soon. If you want to get out and about, this is your chance!" Mary Ryan wiped floured hands on the hem of her apron as she spoke.

"You're right, Mother." Katelyn glanced upward to catch a rear view of her mother returning to the kitchen, knowing full well there would be a set of floured palm prints on the back of her mother's denim skirt. Mrs. Ryan had never been able to bake pies without powdering the kitchen and herself as well.

"Arne called while you were napping." Mary's voice filtered from the kitchen. "He and Jean were wondering if you'd join them at the pitchfork fondue tonight before the musical. I told him you'd call when you woke up."

Katelyn yawned and stretched on the floral velveteen couch. She *had* slept the day away. On purpose. It was easier than remembering those unwelcome emotions Luke Stanton had awakened in her last night. It would be difficult to keep a man at arm's length if in his arms was where she desired to be.

"Perhaps it's because he looks so much like the

Marquis de Mores," Katelyn muttered as she slipped off the couch.

"Who looks like the marquis?" Mary stood in the living room doorway, hands on her hips.

"Mama! You startled me! I thought you'd gone to the kitchen!"

"Don't be putting me off, Katelyn. Who looks like the marquis?"

"Luke Stanton. Haven't you seen the resemblance?"

"He does indeed. Even more so when he's in costume for the musical. He does the stunt riding for those little pageants they do on the cliffs above the amphitheater stage. It's like a dream come true for you, Katelyn." Her eyes danced mischievously.

"Now, Mother…"

"Oh, I remember you mooning about the house for years, reading books about the Marquis de Mores and Medora, talking about how romantic their lives must have been. I was the only mother in town grateful when my daughter laid down the history books and started taking an interest in boys!"

"I finally decided I'd never find a man as dashing as the marquis and that I might have to settle for Jimmy Souders!" She smiled with her mother.

"And now there's one living here in Medora."

Katelyn glanced upward sharply. Luke Stanton was hardly a dream come true. Just a man. And men had turned her dreams to nightmares before.

"I think I'll go to the pitchfork fondue with Arne and Jean. It's been years. I'll call and tell them I'll meet them on the bluff."

Arne and Jean were already at the fondue by the time Katelyn arrived. She'd taken time to pull on fresh jeans and a heavy woolen sweater. Night winds in Medora carried a chilly bite.

The fondue was in progress. Workers were dipping large roasts impaled on the tines of pitchforks into oil bubbling in barrels over a fire. When the meat was cooked, it was carved and served to the waiting line of diners.

"Hello, there! Are you ready to eat?" Arne already had a big stack of plates and napkins in one hand.

Katelyn shivered a bit as a gust of wind swirled about her, but she nodded. Then, suddenly, her appetite was gone.

Across the windy plateau, lounging at a wooden table, was Luke—with a bevy of attractive young women. As she watched, two more men joined the group, but to Katelyn it seemed that Luke was the women's prime attraction. He sat with one hip on the edge of the table, his left leg bent to rest his foot on the bench beneath. The wind ruffled the dark hair and the flaps of his black Western jacket. And he was laughing.

Obviously at ease, he looked relaxed—and susceptible to feminine charms. A slim woman in brief white shorts and a revealing cutout T-shirt was plying her wiles, edging closer and closer to the curve of Luke's arm. He turned occasionally from his conversation to smile at her.

Numbly, Katelyn allowed Arne and Jean to press her into line for supper. A single thought ran rampant in her mind. *He's no different from Randy after all!*

"Katelyn, are you all right?" Arne's rotund face peered into hers. "You look awfully pale."

"I'm fine. I was just thinking."

"About the past?" His eyes were so round and sympathetic that Katelyn offered him a fragment of the secret she'd so far kept hidden.

"About one of the reasons I broke off my engagement."

"Is it something you want to talk about?"

"Not really. It's still pretty fresh. My fiancé...Randy ...had another woman."

A flash of anger flickered across Arne's normally placid features, but Katelyn stilled it with a gentle hand on his arm.

"It was better to find out before we were married, Arne. It just hurts sometimes, that's all."

"I'm so sorry, Katelyn," her friend sputtered, for once at a loss for words.

"So am I, Arne. But I'll get over it. Come on, we're getting close to the food!" She nodded toward the buffet. It would be useless to tell him more, to tell him she had been little more than an attractive coverup for Randy's illegal dealings and that she refused to be hurt again.

Just as her plate was full, the object of her real speculations caught her eye across the hard-packed bluff. Luke's eyes lit with pleasure, and she watched him excuse himself from the group and move toward her.

"Hello. It's nice to see you here tonight. Are you going to the musical?"

"Yes." She settled herself at a picnic table, feigning more nonchalance than she felt. "Arne and Jean asked me to come." She glanced about for her friends only to discover they were deep in conversation with a group sitting near the fondue. Intuitively she knew she'd been abandoned when Luke made his presence known.

"Fine friends they are," she muttered under her breath. They were a useless protection against Luke if they continued their blatant matchmaking.

Looking amused, he slipped onto the bench across

from her. But before he could speak, she said, "Don't worry about me. They'll be over in a minute to keep me company. You shouldn't leave your...friends...like that."

He chuckled. "I see more than enough of my 'friends,' Katelyn. That's part of the cast from the musical. If I have anything I want to say to them, I can do it between scenes."

"Oh." She should have thought of that. Jealousy could do insidious things to logic. And she had no right or reason to be jealous. "Those women are very attractive."

"I suppose they are," he nodded agreeably, doing nothing to tranquilize the little green monster in her skull.

"You suppose so? I would have thought a red-blooded American male like yourself would know for sure!" Katelyn was dumbfounding even herself. But the idea of Luke and all those actresses together for hours on end became an irritation she couldn't suppress.

"Actually, I prefer redheads to blonds and brunettes. Otherwise I'd still be over there instead of here with you." Luke smiled as he spoke. She had the feeling she'd made it clear that jealousy was nipping at her insides. She felt absolutely transparent under Luke's steady gaze. She saw, gratefully, that his eyes were understanding—and kind.

"I'm sorry. I had no right to snipe. I'm just feeling a bit lonely and out of place. I never dreamed that would be possible in Medora. I just don't know many people out here tonight."

"But you should know better than anyone that the majority of the work force changes here every summer. Out with the old college kids, in with the new."

56

He shifted on the bench, leaning forward on his elbows until their faces were very near.

"Somehow I had myself convinced that everything had frozen like a still photo, just waiting for me to return. Unrealistic, I know. Mother wrote when Jake died this spring, but I really didn't believe it until I saw your new cabin with Gus snoring on the porch."

He nodded and his eyes creased into a multitude of agreeable smile lines. "I'm sorry if I'm a shock after Jake, but I hope the cabin is an improvement."

"Especially the bathtub," she agreed, suddenly more cheerful. "What made you decide to come to Medora, Luke?"

His eyes darkened thoughtfully. "The scenery, the chance to own my own business, the adventure."

"Then you *are* a bit like the Marquis de Mores!"

He groaned audibly and ran lean fingers through his dark hair. "That reminds me! I have to go get dressed for the musical. Can I see you later?" Katelyn's internal battle must have flashed across her features as well, for Luke added, "Please?"

Disarmed, she found herself nodding, doing the very thing she had vowed she wouldn't. She was rewarded with a smile as broad as those she'd seen him bestowing on his friends across the bluff.

"Good! I'll have my horses saddled for the performance. How about a moonlight ride to return them to the stable?"

She winced. "My hips and legs are just beginning to recover from our last ride, Luke. I'm a greenhorn now—not used to hours in the saddle." When she'd awakened this morning, her hips felt as if they'd been flogged. Only the day's activities had eased her stiffness.

"Then a ride is the best remedy. See you after the

show." He uncoiled from the bench and made his way toward the cast and crew, unconscious of the appealing sight he made in his dusty Western garb.

As Luke departed, Arne and Jean reappeared.

"It's almost miraculous the way you two appear and disappear, depending on Luke Stanton's whereabouts," Katelyn chided.

"You should be thanking us, my dear. It wasn't easy not to keep you for ourselves. Luke is the only man I'd allow to push me out of the picture."

"Don't you just love Luke, Katelyn?" Jean enthused. "He's so...well, sexy!"

"Jean!" Arne bleated, half in jest and half in dismay.

"Well, he is. Katelyn can see it. She's not blind." Then she turned to her red-faced husband. "Not that we don't love you, of course. There's something very appealing about an...ample man." She patted her husband's rotund tummy.

Choking back laughter, Katelyn turned to seek out Luke's dark head, but he had departed with the crew. The wind whipped about her back, and she shivered. Having been oblivious to the cool breezes while she was with Luke, she now felt suddenly robbed of warmth. Steady and warming as the sun, Luke allayed her doubts and fears. But the moment he was gone, the old ghost returned.

"Katelyn, are you coming?"

Arne and Jean had risen and were waiting patiently for her to join them. The fondue crowd was no longer milling about but edging toward the amphitheater. The musical was about to begin.

The hard-packed earth and manmade steps edged precipitously downward into the seating area. The stage was at the base of the theater with seats built into the sloping walls. On both sides of the stage rose the bluffs, and behind the backdrops the terraced hills of the Badlands extended as far as the eye could see. The arena filled rapidly, and Katelyn again marveled at the numbers of tourists the little cowtown attracted.

Soon she was caught up in the spectacle and the music. As portions of Medora's history were re-enacted, Katelyn would catch glimpses of Luke—in Theodore Roosevelt's wild ride up San Juan hill, as the marquis, and finally, as an outlaw who once rode the hills.

He was riding Midnight. The horse seemed restive beneath him, barely in control. Then just as the song crescendoed, a shot rang out. Luke arched in the saddle as though the force of the bullet propelled him forward. Midnight's wild forefeet pawing the air above him, he tumbled to the ground and rolled limply down the steep and rocky incline—dead.

Katelyn felt a scream of terror rise in her throat as she scanned the lower cliffs for Luke's body. Suddenly, thunderous clapping jarred her back to reality.

Heart hammering in her chest, she heard Arne's voice. "Are you okay? You jumped like *you'd* been shot!"

Feeling vaguely silly at becoming so engrossed in Luke's performance, she replied, "It was so real! I'd forgotten how involved I could become. For a minute I thought…"

"We all know about you and history, Katelyn. But don't get too lost in it. I have a feeling your present-day cowboy will be out here to look for you soon. Jean and I will be moseying along now. Do you think you can find your way home with Luke?"

Chagrined at how confidently they assumed she would wait for Luke, she nodded. Was she really so transparent? She watched the last of the crowd filing upward toward the arena's exit. As she hung back, butterflies flitted nervously in her midsection. Feeling very young and awkward, she made patterns in the dirt with her toe and wished Luke would hurry.

"Boo!"

Katelyn felt Luke's hands slip about her waist just as she heard the soft breathy utterance near her ear. Still, she jumped like a skittish colt and nearly tumbled backward into his arms.

"You frightened me!"

"Sorry. Weren't you expecting me?"

"Up on the bluff, I mean. For a minute I thought someone *had* shot you. Where did you learn to act like that?"

"No acting. Just imagining what it would be like to be shot off my horse. I worked out rolling down the hill without killing myself on my own. Self-preservation. If I didn't twist and turn just right, I'd tear myself to shreds." He lowered his voice as he leaned toward her. "Tough way to make a buck, wouldn't you say? I'm just lucky I share this job with another rider. I only get shot dead three nights a week."

He was so near she could see every movement of his lips and eyes. Mingled with the familiar smell of soap and aftershave was the dry, powdery smell of dust, and she moved to wipe a smear from his cheek.

But he turned his head and kissed the palm of her hand. Katelyn's throat constricted. Where were all those thorny defenses she'd erected?

Instead, in her mind's eye she could imagine them standing there in the empty amphitheater, herself slim and red-haired, Luke angular and dark, so much like the marquis of long ago. De Mores and his beloved Medora, Luke and Katelyn, so much a part of these hills.

She felt a sharp pang of kinship. Luke was like the embodiment of a dream. For a moment, she imagined herself in Medora von Hoffman's shoes, here in the bewildering and chaotic beauty of a wild and mysterious land, with the man she loved.

Impulsively, she leaned toward Luke, her lips inviting his kiss. She could see the pleased glow in his eye as he willingly acquiesced to her dreamy demand. She could taste the chalky dust on his lips and the warm sweetness of his mouth.

"When you two are through smooching, I'm going to turn out the lights!" A disembodied voice floated down from the top of the amphitheater.

Katelyn felt Luke's body tremble with a light chuckle as he reluctantly pulled away from her.

"I think that's a hint that they want to close up shop. Are you ready for that moonlight ride?"

Still besotted with the taste and smell of him, she followed him through the backstage jumble to where Midnight and Wildfire were grazing on a sparse patch of brush.

"Up you go." He boosted her into the saddle and turned to his own mount. She was sorry when his hands left the trim hollow of her waist.

In the darkness she felt disembodied and free. For the first time in months, she recognized some of her former lighthearted nature returning. Something in Luke's steady strength reassured her that all *could* be right with the world and she felt secure in his presence.

Those sweet thoughts lingered as they moved out into the moonlight. Luke was characteristically silent, and the only sound was the ringing of their horses' hooves as they wound their way into the hills.

The clatter of hooves ceased as they reined in to gaze over the vast parcel of Badlands, rent and torn by river and fire, full of ragged gorges, towering buttes, and gaping chasms. From the tablelands in moonlight, the terrain looked like the lost ruins of a great and ancient city, the skeletal structure of a former empire.

Finally, Luke spoke. "When I look across the Badlands at night, when I can only see what the moon illuminates, I always think of ancient Rome."

Amazed, Katelyn breathed, "You've been there, then? To Rome, I mean?"

He laughed softly. "In the same way your father's been to Ireland, Katelyn. In my head. In my books. But someday I'll go. Some winter when the tourists are gone and the horses are cared for. It's something to work toward."

"Is that your goal in life, then? To travel?" Her horse did an impatient jig, edging her even closer to Luke's side. Moonlight illuminated the exquisite angles in the planes of his face.

He turned then and studied her intently, as if weighing the question. Katelyn's stomach did a flip-flop. His evaluation of her was so intense, she felt his answer had to be of monumental importance.

"My goals? They're more complex than that, Katelyn. And I'm not sure where life will ultimately take me. As long as I seek God's will for my life, I have to trust that *His* goals for me will be fulfilled."

An odd nervousness trickled through her. That was the last answer she had expected. Earthy, handsome, *sexy* Luke Stanton—a Christian?

He was studying her again, obviously waiting for a reaction. He had waited this long to say anything, she was sure, because he expected her response to be negative. And he was right. Talk of religion made her vaguely uncomfortable. History was one thing. The hocus-pocus of religion was quite another.

"Luke..."

"You don't have to say anything, Katelyn. I know how you feel. Your father and I have had long talks about the very subject you're trying to avoid. I know Ben's feelings about my faith, and I suspect yours are the same. I know how much you admire your father and his opinions."

But what had her father said about Luke? Katelyn thought back to their discussion in the kitchen over lunch. So this is what her father had meant! To think of Luke as…religious—she grudgingly had to formulate the distasteful word in her mind—was surprising indeed.

"But maybe that's not what you wanted to know about me, Katelyn." He was speaking again, humor apparent in his voice. "When you ask me about life's purposes and goals, that's what you get. Ask me something about my work and you'll hear nothing but horses. Is that more comfortable territory?"

Gratefully, she realized he was letting her off the hook. At least he wasn't one of those religious zealots who appalled her!

"I do believe I'd rather discuss horses tonight, Luke," she hedged, struggling to keep her voice even. There was no need to hurt his feelings just because she didn't agree with him. And a moonlit night was too precious to waste arguing theology. "What did you do all day long?"

"Besides swing a pitchfork and mend saddles you mean? Are you wondering about the exciting life I lead? Today is a good day to ask. I had more excitement today than I care to have again for a long time."

"And just what does that mean?"

Luke was staring across the dimly lit hills and into the distance. "I just don't understand how people can take this place so much for granted, how they can be so…careless."

"Luke?"

He was obviously upset. The stamping and pawing of the horse beneath him mirrored the turmoil in his features.

"I took the Jeep out today, just to look around. I pulled into the camping area as a family was about to leave. They'd left a poorly doused fire smouldering and were ready to drive away. I had to stop them and point out what they'd done."

"And they didn't take it well?" She could picture the scene. She'd been with her father on several occasions when he'd had to chastise tourists for their carelessness.

"Not at all. The man told me off in language I haven't heard since my days in the Navy." He grinned wryly. "The air was blue for a mile in every direction."

"Apparently he didn't think he would be responsible for any fires that might start as a result of his carelessness."

"He didn't think at all. Before he was done, his wife and kids were standing behind him—all reading me the riot act for interfering in their lives. And the entire time that fire was smouldering behind them. They obviously haven't seen what a fire can do in dry grass."

"Is the area dry this spring?"

"More than usual. Normally the danger of fire is worst in August. Then the vegetation is pure tinder. But it's been dry this spring. A fire could move through pretty quickly. I had no choice, but I still didn't enjoy the confrontation."

She nodded in sympathetic understanding. She'd grown up steeped in a love for this wild land of precipitous gorges and weird formations. It was difficult to understand someone who couldn't respect its beguiling beauty.

Suddenly, from nowhere, came a blood-congealing cry. Katelyn stiffened in the saddle as Wildfire danced.

"Coyotes," Luke commented, squinting into the darkness.

"Brrrr, I don't like that sound. Let's get out of here."

His chuckle replaced the haunting keen of the creature. "Come on, city woman, let's ride through town on the way to your house. The wildest thing there is a tourist who's spent too much time at the saloon."

Willingly, she followed his lead. They rode by the eastern wall of the town, a cliff of yellow-gold rock. The little hamlet nestled against it, secure in the arm of the rocky fortress.

Her imagination roamed as she stared at the craggy rock, picturing the faces of the past etched in the imposing wall of stone. Her eyes sought the crevices and crannies for the weathered profiles of an Indian chief or the furrowed brow and piercing eye of the buffalo hunter. Since childhood, she had looked for the forms of the past in these timeless rocks.

And again, she appreciated Luke's companionable silence. He rode loosely in the saddle, as much a part of the beast as a man could be. His back was ramrod straight, his thighs thick with muscles, and his shoulders rolled imperceptibly under the dirt-smudged shirt. Then he reined in his horse and turned to look at her across his shoulder.

"Coming?"

"Uh-huh. I was just watching you ride." She nudged her horse forward with the heels of her boots.

His teeth flashed white in the light of the street lamp. "We're not *that* desperate for entertainment in Medora, are we?"

"I was rather enjoying it, actually. You ride very well."

"Practice. Years of practice. I have to stay in the saddle from morning until night just to stay in shape."

"Quit teasing me, Luke. How long have you been riding? Really?"

"Since I was five. I got my first pony for my fifth birthday, and I've never walked when I could ride since. It's made a lazy man of me, Katelyn.

"Here we are." His voice held a tinge of regret as they came upon Ben Ryan's bungalow. The kitchen light was gleaming through ruffled cafe curtains, casting an orange and white shadow into the night.

He leaned forward, and Katelyn felt him grasp the reins and tug her animal closer to his own mount.

"What are you do...?" The words were lost as he leaned to kiss her, his lips grazing hers, light as birds' wings on the air. She felt a shiver of excitement shimmy down her spine, and she leaned into the feathery kiss, hungry for more. Her mount shuddered beneath her, and she could feel Wildfire flick his tail, ridding himself of a pesky fly. The two beasts swayed beneath them and finally danced apart, impatient with the gentle ritual of the riders on their backs.

Luke was the first to speak. "I suppose this is why people seldom take horses on dates anymore. It's easier to kiss in a car."

Katelyn giggled. "I see my father peering out the kitchen window. While I was growing up he probably wished for more young men who would ask me to go riding and fewer who had kissing in mind."

"Tell Ben I'm old enough to supervise myself now, thank you. It's been a long time since a worried father watched me kiss my date good night."

Suddenly she envied the young women she imagined Luke had known. He'd come into her own life too late. The naive trust she had once shown was gone, irreplaceably shattered. She swung to the ground and handed him Wildfire's reins.

Tipping his hat, he said softly, "G'night, Katelyn. Sleep well." To the accompaniment of muffled hoof beats, he disappeared into the night.

Chapter Five

Katelyn awoke smiling. The memory of a goodnight kiss from the swaying, shuddering backs of Midnight and Wildfire teased alight a small flame in her midsection.

Those restless, stomping creatures had made the kiss a game of chance. But Luke had been lucky. Was it a gamester's good luck or the magnetism of her lips so eagerly wanting his?

She sensed a thawing in emotions she was sure had turned to glacial ice. Perhaps she *was* ready to gamble on love again.

"Are you awake in there, Katelyn? There's some mail for you." Mary Ryan's voice drifted through the door. "Chicago postmarks."

Katelyn winced and buried her head in her pillow. Chicago. Some of the happy glow faded as she scrambled from the bed. When she arrived in the kitchen, she was still buttoning the cracked buttons of her old chambray work shirt and stuffing the tail into wash-faded jeans.

"My, but you've adapted well to our lifestyle," her mother commented, eyeing the faded work clothes and riot of uncombed red hair.

Katelyn chuckled and plucked a fresh roll from the heaping plate on the table. Her mother poured steaming black coffee into a chipped souvenir mug and pushed it toward her daughter.

"I'll never be away from Medora long enough to forget how much I love it here. I know I look like a refugee from a ragbag, but tomorrow I have to cinch myself into a long dress and petticoats. Today is my day to relax."

"Anything special planned?" Mary gave her a sly look.

"No, Mother, nothing special," Katelyn chided, knowing her mother wanted to ask if Luke Stanton fit into the day. It was a question she had already considered herself.

"You'd better look at your mail. They must have forwarded a whole bundle at once." Mrs. Ryan handed Katelyn a stack of letters.

"Thanks. Let's see who's taken time to write." She flipped through the pile, checking return addresses. "My boss. My friend Angie. The phone company. Three department stores. Randy…"

Randy! She stared at the familiar handwriting. Revulsion, confusion, and dismay flooded her. But another trickle of emotion followed the torrent. Love. She *had* loved him—or come as close to that sentiment as she ever had. Then he had used her, deceived her. Betrayed, she had run away—run from the source of her pain and from love itself.

Her jaw squared in renewed determination. She had unwittingly been lulled into lowering her guard. Luke Stanton with his understanding silences and easy smiles had made her think of loving again. The arrival of Randy's letter would save her from making that drastic mistake.

"Did you say Randy?" Mrs. Ryan bustled toward the table.

"I did, Mother, but I'm sure it's nothing. Maybe I'll just go out on the steps to read my mail. Do you mind?"

"Of course not. Do whatever you please. Tomorrow is soon enough for schedules."

Gratefully Katelyn fled the kitchen. Her mother had shown great restraint in refraining from questions about Randy. It would be unkind to test her any further. Katelyn knew she was not ready to reveal the entire story to her parents. Not yet.

She pulled a red bandana from her hip pocket and wound it about her neck, tucking the knotted ends under her shirt collar. Then she dusted a spot on the redwood steps and settled against the silvered porch railing. Now there was nothing left to do but open the letter.

The deep angles and pitches of Randy's familiar scrawl had not changed. A fine gold necklace slithered out of the envelope with the brief note.

Katelyn–

I know you didn't want to hear from me, but even I'm not such a creep that I'd keep your grandmother's necklace. You must have put it in my coat pocket when the clasp broke. I know how sentimental you are.

Too bad you got hooked up with the likes of me. Maybe country girls should stay on the farm where they belong.

Sorry it all worked out this way, Katelyn. Guess it's really true what they say—"Crime doesn't pay." But it was worth a try—

Randy

Bold, unrepentant Randy. She fingered the fine gold strand. She had been sure she would never see it again. There *was* some small humane streak in Randy after all. She'd not been entirely wrong in her judgment. *Just an innocent country girl.*

"Not anymore, Randy Baker! Not anymore!" She spoke aloud, her voice ringing across the porch. Furious with the naive young woman she had been and brimming with pent-up anger, she tucked her mail under the steps and jogged toward the center of town.

Her anger subsided as she neared the Rough Rider. Arne and Jean were just leaving the cafe.

"Hello there, Katelyn. Misplace your horse or did you decide to go for a gallop without it?"

"Hi," she panted in reply. "I needed the exercise. Did I miss morning coffee?"

"I'm afraid so. Jean and I are driving to Bismarck today or we'd join you anyway. But," Arne said with a sly smile, "Luke usually has the coffeepot on up at his cabin. He's probably better company, too. I'd wager his arthritis didn't keep him awake last night."

"Thanks, but no thanks, Cupid. I'll just pass for this morning. Have a good trip to the big city."

Waving good-bye, Katelyn felt a surge of loneliness crest and break over her. Feeling perversely abandoned, she made her way to the city's limits. It was not until she saw the first ramshackle barn of the stables that she realized where her impertinent feet were taking her.

Drawn like a bee to pollen, she was edging toward the riding stable. Against her better judgment and the

71

warning light flashing in her brain, she followed the winding footpath to Luke's cabin.

The air was already hot and dry. An occasional whiff of malodorous dust stung her nostrils, as if the breeze had taken a turn through some sealed and ancient attic. She was reminded of Luke's comment about the dangerous and unseasonable dryness of the hills.

Luke was not at the cabin, giving her the opportunity to think about what she was doing. Though she was still snapping with unresolved hostility toward Randy and males in general, Katelyn had felt unaccountably drawn to see Luke again, to seek out his calm, nonjudgmental presence.

"Maybe it's that Christianity thing," she muttered. Perhaps that was what separated him from the others in her mind. Nonsense though it might be, it seemed unlikely that anyone professing those ideals would betray her as Randy had. And Luke listened to her, really listened, as no one else ever had. She found herself disappointed when the tack room, too, was empty.

"Get off my foot, big fella!" Luke's voice drifted from the far end of the corral.

She smiled, half relieved, half amused. Luke seemed to be having troubles of his own.

"Need some help?" She sauntered toward the voice, which seemed to have emanated from a cluster of saddled ponies. A single pair of jean-clad legs was visible from beneath the bellies of the beasts.

"You bet." Luke's head popped up over the top of a saddle. He was being buffeted about by curious noses. "I made the mistake of bringing some apples out here. Now they won't leave me alone, and I still have eight horses to saddle!"

"Looks like the whole bunch is ready for a trail ride."

"I have three large families coming in. They're having a reunion here, and they all want to go out together. I overslept this morning and now I'm really in a fix. The fellow I've hired to help me had a dental appointment somewhere, and I'm doing this one alone." He slapped the hindquarters of a lustrous filly as he spoke.

"Can you use some help?"

"Sure can." He grinned broadly. "Front or rear?"

"Front or rear what?" She glanced suspiciously at the horse.

"You can either lead the trail ride or bring up the rear. Maybe you'd better take the lead. Just give Wildfire her head and she'll do the rest. I'll ride last just to speed up the straggling ponies and keep the old-timers from stopping to graze. Thanks, Katelyn."

"Any time." And much to her surprise, she meant it. Already she was feeling better. Even if she didn't want any more romantic entanglements in her life, she did want Luke for a friend.

"How are you at saddling a horse?"

"Poor, but maybe you can teach me."

"I've got Lightfoot and Manitou left to do, plus as many of the other six as I can manage before the families arrive."

"Why do those names sound familiar?" she inquired, her curiosity piqued.

"I'm impressed! No one else has ever recognized them."

"Then tell me why they're familiar. Don't keep me in the dark!"

"Those were the names of Theodore Roosevelt's horses when he lived here in Medora. I thought it would be a nice touch to have some namesakes here at

73

the stable. But you're the first one who's caught on to it."

"Here they come, Luke! Carloads of them! Are we ready?" She watched a curious crowd pour out of panel-sided station wagons.

He sighed, thrusting forward his lower lip and blowing aside a strand of dark hair that had fallen in his eyes. "Just pray that none of them thinks he's a stunt rider and takes any foolish chances on one of my horses." He paused for a moment before adding, "Well, here we go."

Katelyn watched his denim-covered back disappear into the crowd of pastel polo shirts. He'd sounded halfway serious. "I suppose there are more foolish things to pray for!" she murmured aloud as she spied a little boy nearing the hooves of a spirited horse. If his only experience with a horse was the television set, this could prove a perilous introduction.

She marveled at Luke's patience as he matched rider to mount, hoisting body after unaccustomed body into the saddle. The smile on his face never wavered, and his charm never faltered, even when the matriarch of the clan pitched backward with one foot in the stirrup. Even tall, muscular Luke staggered under her bulk, but he calmly uprighted her and encouraged her back toward the saddle.

"Are you ready?" He came up behind Katelyn on a trim red filly.

Her mount was restive from the wait and danced beneath her, the big body rolling and churning impatiently. "Just say when. Are you sure this horse knows the way?"

"He's done it hundreds of times. Just don't let him take it too fast. Everyone wants to look around on the ride. Besides that, not one person in this group has ever been on a horse before. I feel like I've already put in a full day's work."

Beads of perspiration stood out on his forehead, glistening in the late-morning sun. A T-shaped pattern of sweat pasted his shirt to his back, and his jeans and boots were covered with a fine powder of ashen dirt. And three middle-aged women were waving their arms in the air, vying for his attention.

"No wonder you like that bathtub," Katelyn commented softly, so no one else could hear.

He grinned engagingly. "Oh, how I'd love to take a dip right now! But duty calls. Pull out, Katelyn. And by the way," he called back over his shoulder, "when we come to the water, just let the horses gallop on through. It's so low they won't even get their bellies wet. Give our riders a thrill."

With only a nudge of her stirrups they were on their way, winding single file into the hills of the Badlands, edging nearer the sun. When Katelyn turned in the saddle to look back at the snaking procession, she could see Luke moving back and forth along the line, prodding a horse who wanted to graze, encouraging a frightened rider.

Lost in the beauty of the landscape, Katelyn watched the colors of the land. Horizontal bands of multihued clays and scoria made the hills oddly striped in ochre, gray, red, brown, and pink. Black veins of lignite shot through the water-washed hills, barren and stark against the azure sky. An occasional patch of fertile soil produced feathers of prairie grass and tenacious cedar clung to the muted buttes in bright green contrast.

As the group reached the pinnacle of their ride and could look out across the hills in a great circle, Katelyn thought of the old-timer who had compared this land to a great rag rug, woven of all kinds and colors of rags. It was simple, homely, and yet spectacularly beautiful.

As they neared the stable at ride's end, the horses began to perk up their ears and lift their hooves higher, eager for home and their nightly rations.

"Nice job, Katelyn." Luke swung onto the corral fence next to her, still waving good-bye to the last of the wood-paneled station wagons. He scrubbed his face with the blue bandana handkerchief from his hip pocket, having dipped it in the murky depths of the horses' water tank. His skin glistened like grass heavy with morning dew.

"You're a wonder, Luke Stanton."

"I am? And just what are you wondering?"

"You know what I mean. How you kept your patience through all that nonsense I'll never know. Those horses were jabbed in the sides and jerked in the mouths until they should have bucked the whole crew into oblivion."

"I'm a patient man, Katelyn. Usually. But there are some things I have trouble waiting for."

"What do you have trouble waiting for, Luke?"

"This." He leaned closer, his eyes intent, and took her chin in his hand, running his long fingers from the curve of her jawbone to the curve of her chin. Gently he drew her face to meet his own and lowered his lips to hers. The heady, masculine smells of leather, horseflesh, and musk hypnotized her. His lips, dry from the gusty breezes and pounding sun, traced a pattern across her own, eking from them the very response she had vowed not to give. She surrendered and leaned forward, carelessly jeopardizing her perch on the top fence rail.

"Delicious." He pulled away, smiling, licking his lips

76

as though he had just tasted sweet wild honey. "I had good reason to be impatient."

"Luke…" she began. She was ready to be his friend, but she was not prepared for the promises their kisses held.

Suddenly, a blaring horn intruded into their moment, pulling their eyes toward the dusty road.

A young woman, one of the just-departed riding party, flung herself from the station wagon, screaming.

"My baby! Have you seen my baby?" Wild-eyed and incoherent, she barreled toward the couple on the fence. She clutched at Luke's arm as he dismounted the railing.

"Whoa, whoa, there. I'm not sure what baby it is you're looking for. There weren't any babies on the ride."

"He's not a baby, Martha; he's three years old." Her husband approached, an impatient whine coloring his voice. "Excuse us, sir, my wife thought Billy was with me and I thought he was with her.…we were both wrong."

Luke turned to Katelyn. "Go to the cabin and call for help. We'll look around the buildings while we're waiting for some more manpower. The horses are all still saddled, so we can take them and fan out in a circle. How far can a three-year-old go in two hours?"

His mistake was in asking the question, for the terrified Martha set up a pitiful wail. Katelyn had read the fear in Luke's own eyes. The Badlands were no place for anyone to be lost—certainly not a child.

She returned with her report in a flash. "There's a group checking around town, Luke, and the rest will be here shortly." Her eyes widened as he strapped a gun belt about his hips and secured the holster thong

77

above the knee. A hunting knife protruded from his belt.

"Luke?" she hissed.

The winter in his eyes frightened her. "Just a precaution. The child could toddle into most anything out there. A cranky badger or ferret, maybe."

"Or a rattler?"

"That, too. Are you going to stay here or ride?

"Ride. I've got good eyesight." She knew how difficult a small child would be to spot if he'd tumbled into one of the ravines. According to his mother, the boy was dressed in khaki and green—Badlands colors, an unfortunate choice. But he was carrying a red clown doll.

"Then ride with me. I see the others are arriving."

She turned to watch the men congregate, somber and determined. If this crew couldn't locate the boy, no one could. Spinning back to Luke, she found him, his arm resting across the rear jockey and skirt of the saddle, and his head bent into the crook of his arm. His eyes were closed.

"Luke? Luke?" She moved toward him, shielding his posture from the rest of the group, afraid he was ill.

Lifting his head, he smiled at her, a clear, penetrating, unwavering smile.

"Luke, what were you do—" And then it dawned on her. He had been praying! Uncomfortable at interrupting such a private moment, she began to back away, but his voice stopped her.

Unembarrassed, he made no apology. "I'm not sure we'll find him on our own, Katelyn. This is God's own maze of crevices and crannies. I think we'd better go to the Maker for help."

Silently, she nodded. For once she could agree. They needed all the help they could get.

The group fanned out from the stables in a concentric circle, like ripples on water, slowly spreading across the sharp inclines, calling the child's name.

"Jason! Jason!" The name rang through the unanswering hills.

Luke and Katelyn took the path they had followed both hours and eons before on the trail ride. Their eyes scanned the landscape for a tiny figure with butterscotch curls and a red clown doll.

"Too much color." Growing fear was making Katelyn's conversation clipped. "The colors change with the movement of the sun and every passing cloud. The landscape keeps changing, Luke! How will we ever find him?"

"We will. And remind me never to let another customer go on a ride without signing a statement that they haven't left any of their children behind. What do those people use for brains? Oatmeal?" Luke reined in and stood in the stirrups, perusing the clay-baked buttes. "No wonder outlaws used to come here to hide. I never realized what a convenient place to lose yourself this is.

"All the things that make this a good place for cattle make it a rotten place for a child to be lost. These cuts and shallow ravines are good shelter but difficult to follow. We'll have to hope he'll answer if someone calls to him. At least the vegetation isn't high and the wa—" Luke bit at his lower lip and settled himself into the saddle.

"Water? Is that what you were going to say, Luke? The water?" A new fear settled about Katelyn's shoulders like a shroud. Drowning was another way to die in the Badlands.

Her thighs felt as though they were being torn from their sockets. She and Luke had wound their way

79

through cuts and ravines, urging the horses beyond their limits.

Finally Luke spoke. "He couldn't have come any farther than this. I couldn't have done it on foot. If he's on the land we crossed over, we've missed him. The shadings and shadows will be different on the way back. We've got to turn around."

Their hopeful silence was soon replaced by the heavy cloak of despair. The landscape she loved seemed tainted now. The wild montage of cliffs and ravines held a hint of death. She would have exchanged all of the peaceful silence for the cry of a child.

"Katelyn, look!" Luke jerked so hard on his reins that Wildfire reared skyward. His eyes were riveted to a spot of red protruding from a scraggly shrub. He swung his leg over the saddle and skidded toward the scrap, his high-heeled boots digging into the earth. He came back to her slowly, a small clown doll, its plastic face scratched and dented, in his outstretched hand.

"He's here! He's got to be." Katelyn swung off her horse to join Luke on the ground and stood scanning the landscape.

"And he can't be far. It must have taken him a good hour to work his way here. I'd bet my shirt that he's sound asleep somewhere nearby. You go that way, and I'll circle around in the other direction."

Cupping her hands to her mouth, Katelyn sang into the gusting breeze, "Jason! Jason!" Trudging uphill through the rough brush, she wondered at how the little fellow could have made it this far.

"Mama?"

Katelyn halted. The wind whipped at her back, snapping the shirttail that had worked its way free of her waistband. Was her hopeful imagination playing tricks?

"Mama?"

"Jason!" She screamed until the tender inner flesh of her throat threatened to tear, but there was no answer.

"Did you find him?" Luke had come up behind her, and she jumped as his hand touched her shoulder. She'd forgotten all but the child.

"He's here somewhere. I heard him say, 'Mama.' But now he won't answer."

Luke's eyes darted across the jagged terrain. "If you can hear him, he's nearby, behind one of these knolls or rocks. Get him to answer you one more time, and I can find him."

"Jason! Mama wants you!" she cajoled as loudly as the wind and her tortured throat would allow.

"Mama?"

"Okay. I can get him." Luke scrabbled up the incline and disappeared behind a knotted chunk of earth. Seconds later he was sliding back to her, a wide-eyed, curly-haired toddler in his arms.

Katelyn's shoulders slumped in relief. The wind was whipping up a dusty fury around them. Thousands of specks of sand and gravel assaulted her eyes until they watered. At least that was her excuse for tears.

As they rode nearer the stables, it was apparent the others had given up. Luke's horses were unsaddled and grazing in the pasture. A caravan of cars, including the numerous station wagons, were crowding the driveway.

The milling crowd was circling Jason's parents and it was not until the first bystander heard the dull clop of horses' hooves that anyone noticed Luke and Katelyn approaching.

Jason had fallen asleep in Luke's arms and was draped across the front of the saddle, his head and neck resting on Luke's forearm.

Ben Ryan was the one who sent up the cry. "They found him! They found him!"

The crowd parted and Jason's parents flew toward them, crying and laughing, arms open to the dirty little boy.

The sun was dipping in the west as the last of the cars left the driveway. Exhausted and happy, Katelyn and Luke settled themselves on the cabin's front porch to watch the flames of sunset licking the sky.

"You know, this reminds me of something I've been thinking about all day," he commented, curling one strand of her unruly mane about his finger.

"About Jason and his careless parents?"

"No. About you. You and Medora von Hoffman, the Marquise de Mores."

Katelyn turned to him, amazed. "What in the world are you talking about?" Secretly she was flattered to be associated with the woman she so admired, but she was baffled by Luke's meaning.

"The sun is setting that end of the world on fire. You and Medora have the same color hair, full of flames— the sun personified."

Wondering where the conversation was leading, she savored the gentle tug of his finger as he wound his way into her hair.

"I kept noticing your hair when we were riding. It was like following a burning bush." Then he laughed an embarrassed, disarming laugh. "I usually don't tell people what I'm thinking about. Afraid they'd think I'm crazy. Maybe you do now."

"No. Hardly that. Only a sound mind could have found that child today, Luke. All the others had given up. You were the hero of the hour, you know." Her own heart swelled with pride at having been a part of Luke's determined search. She, too, would have given up if he hadn't so doggedly persevered among those hills.

"If I am, I don't deserve to be. I asked for extra help, Katelyn. And He provided it."

"But Luke..." Katelyn didn't like this idea of giving God all the credit. She'd seen how Luke's persistence paid off. *Luke* had searched until the boy was found, not some supernatural deity.

Regretfully, she felt a curtain fall between them. The closeness they'd shared all day was destroyed by Luke's insistence on a higher power that had come to his aid—and to Jason's.

But after all, it really didn't matter. Luke was nothing more than a friend, a pleasant diversion for the summer. Wistfully, she rose to leave and said goodnight before winding her way back to her parents' home.

Tomorrow would be her first day at the chateau.

Chapter Six

Katelyn was at the chateau long before the first tourist would make his way through the gates and up the incline to the de Mores' mansion. A trickle of perspiration meandered down the collar of her dress, toward the tightly cinched waistband. It would be a hundred and five today. Heat was already lifting from the ground in visible waves, undulating hot spots in the late-morning light.

Rehearsing her patter for the tour groups to come, she strolled through the silent mansion, drifting a light finger across mementos of the past. The brick fireplace in the sitting room loomed over the rest of the furnishings.

She had the urge to press her cheek against its smooth, cool brick. That old fireplace had been clever in theory but a failure in practice. Built at the middle of the house, it was exposed to four rooms with the idea that it would heat them all with a single fire. But brittle cold seeped through every cranny in the outer walls, thwarting the big oven's purpose. There was no way a single burning heat could protect from the chill of a North Dakota winter.

The chateau was decorated with an eclectic mixture

of sturdy utilitarian furniture fashioned from the local cottonwoods and ornate European pieces turned out in rare woods. Lavish Oriental carpets and animal hides covered the floors, and hunting trophies shared the walls with delicate watercolors painted by the marquise. Deer horns, buffalo heads, and Medora's Kurtzman piano amicably cohabited the hunting lodge.

"Brother! What a day! Have you ever felt such heat so early in the spring?" Bitsy Malone poked her head around the door jamb.

"Not that I can remember. I'm not sure I'll make it through. It's been a long time since I gave this tour."

"Katelyn, if the heat cooked your brains like poached eggs, you'd still remember every detail about this place." Bitsy's round cheeks gleamed like polished apples. She was nearly an institution at the chateau, having been a summer guide ever since her husband moved to the hamlet to operate a filling station.

"Speaking of cooked brains, what do we do if someone faints? The air is awfully close in here."

"Maybe we can open some doors to the outside. I always wondered why the marquis made four or five doors into every bedroom on the first floor. Maybe he knew some day we'd need the ventilation."

By day's end Katelyn's dress had plastered itself to her ribcage. Semicircles of perspiration beneath her arms had spread to meet the wetness edging upward from her waist. Both she and Bitsy had discarded their shoes, and Katelyn had pinned her fanning tresses into a loose bun on the top of her head.

The sun personified. If that was how Luke thought of her, then today she must be a blazing fury in his mind. Her head was spinning with the vicious heat as she waved farewell to the day's last tour group.

"How was the first day at work?"

She spun about at the question. Luke was lounging against the porch pillar, looking cool and rested in soft blue denims. The summer heat had wilted Katelyn and frayed her temper, but it had left Luke unscathed.

"Why do you look so cool, calm, and collected? And how did you get up here without my hearing you?"

"I've been at a meeting all day—indoors, with air conditioning. Discussing such exciting things as buffalo roundups and thinning deer herds. Animal resource management plans. Today was the easy part. Implementing comes next. *Then* I get hot and sweaty like you."

"Oh." It was difficult to think of him in such diversified roles. He fit so well on the back of a horse, it was impossible to imagine him anywhere else. She picked up the hem of her skirt and wiped her forehead.

He chuckled at the bare toes protruding beneath the petticoats. "Sit down before you fall down. Bad day?"

"No. Just hot. I was tempted to crawl into the wine cellar to cool off. I smiled and talked as long as I could. Then my face melted. Do I look awful?" She pulled at the damp strands of her hair, and the entire flaming mass tumbled about her shoulders.

"You look just fine. But you're making me feel guilty for being cool all day."

"So, tell me, what else did you discuss at this air-conditioned meeting?" She sank gratefully onto the top step of the porch. As Luke sat down beside her, her warmth suddenly didn't seem to be coming from external sources.

"The park service is going to conduct a resource inventory of the plant life and animals in the park. I'm going to help with the animal count. The goal is to maintain a proper balance in the wildlife and vegetation just as it was in the 1880s when Theodore Roosevelt ranched here. It's a fine line to tread. Once the natural balance is tipped, we may not ever be able to restore the equilibrium."

Katelyn had a flash of respect for him. Like her father, he cared very deeply for this wild land. "How did you get so interested in this, Luke?"

"I have a degree in animal husbandry."

Her eyebrows shot upward. Would the surprises never end? He was far more than the simple cowboy visible at first glance.

"Katelyn, are you ready to leave? Well, hello there!" Bitsy popped from the front door, shoes in hand. "How are you, Luke?"

"Good, Bitsy. And you?" He touched a single finger to the brim of his hat in greeting.

"Thinner. Can't you tell?" She chuckled and patted the quivering roll of flesh at her waist.

"And more beautiful," he added earnestly. Katelyn could see his eyes twinkling from beneath the big hat.

"I love this man, Katelyn! He makes me feel better than anyone else I know." Bitsy tweaked Luke's cheeks between her own dimpled fingers, and he growled a low chuckle deep in his belly. Apparently this scenario had been enacted before. "I just love this man!"

I know what you mean. Katelyn surprised herself with the thought. But before she could pursue it, Luke jumped to his feet.

"My Jeep is in the parking lot. Can I give you frontier beauties a ride home?"

Bitsy shook her head regretfully. "I have my own wheels today. But I saw Katelyn's father drop her off here. I'm sure she'd just love to have a ride."

Matchmaker! Everybody's a matchmaker! But the

resentment barely fluttered today. Katelyn followed Luke to his Jeep.

"Oww! It's like an oven in here." The interior of the Jeep sizzled with absorbed solar rays. She leaned forward, away from the burning black seat.

"It's that way all over. Do your folks have air conditioning?"

"Just a little wall unit. I'm sure it's working overtime today. I can hardly wait to get cleaned up." She plucked at her damp dress.

Luke pulled into the Ryan driveway just as Ben was closing the garage door.

"Howdy, kids. Hot enough for you?" He mopped his brow with a limp handkerchief.

Katelyn skirted the two men and headed for the bathroom. Two minutes more in the cumbersome dress would be two minutes too many.

The men's voices followed her into the house, but she lost track of the conversation as she filled the tub and lowered herself into the soapy depths. She closed her eyes and sank beneath the water, purging herself of the clammy grime of the hilltop. A half-hour passed before she emerged from her watery refresher.

She had forgotten about Luke by the time she strolled casually into the kitchen toweling her auburn curls, wrapped in a pink kimono that waged a fierce battle with the red of her hair.

She ground to a halt as she felt Luke's eyes studying her from wet head to pink-nailed barefoot toes.

"Luke's staying for supper, Katelyn. Isn't that nice?"

"Oh, fine," she stammered, wishing her silken robe had buttons instead of a silver sash. She again felt transparent under Luke's gaze until she realized his eyes had never left her face.

Then she felt a perverse nudge of irritation. Wasn't

he even *interested* in what she looked like? As she turned back to her room to change, she realized what a no-win situation she had created for Luke. Either he behaved like Randy, or he didn't—and she would be critical either way.

Sighing, she pulled a mint sundress over her head. The full skirt allowed her legs to breathe and the bared shoulders kept her neck cool. She walked into the kitchen just as her mother began moving the evening meal from pantry to table.

"Get the salads from the refrigerator, dear, will you? There's potato salad in the red bowl and fruit in the blue."

"Step up to the table, Luke," Ben urged. "I'm looking forward to eating with somebody who has an appetite. These women are always on a diet of some kind."

"The ham is cold, and so are the beans. I didn't think anyone would want me to fire up the oven tonight," Mary explained, pushing a mounded platter toward Luke.

Katelyn grinned to herself. Her parents were more excited to have Luke at their table than she was. Were they matchmaking, too?

"Luke, ah…" Ben faltered, "would you like to say the blessing?"

Katelyn's eyes flew open. She'd never heard a blessing spoken at her parents' table in all her life. Ben Ryan discouraged what he labeled "gobbledygook." And now he was asking Luke to pray? Apparently more things had changed in Medora than she had first suspected!

Easily, and without pretense, Luke prayed. "Father, thank you for this food and these friends. May your blessings be on this gathering tonight. Guide, bless, and heal us, oh Lord, and show us *Your* will for our lives. Amen."

Heal us? Katelyn's eyebrow winged upward in curiosity. Who was sick? Or hurt? Or…in pain…The double-edged blade she'd ignored all day twisted, slicing away her cultivated pretense. *She* was in pain. That's who. Mentally. Emotionally. Spiritually?

Could Luke see through the lighthearted banter that deceived the rest? He seemed to know very well who needed healing. Odd, dear, perceptive man. He thought the answer was God and God's will for her life. Naive but sweet.

The corners of her lips lifted. She'd never met a man so full of contrasts—rugged and tender, sexy and spiritual. He was one contradiction after another.

Ben Ryan's contemplative gaze pulled Katelyn from her reverie. A blush rose unbidden to her cheeks.

"Katelyn, don't just sit there daydreaming. Pass Luke the ham."

Her fork clattered to the earthenware plate, sure that the grins on her parents' faces proved they had guessed the reason for her distraction.

"Is it very dry in the park, Ben?" Luke inquired between mouthfuls of pie. Mary Ryan's dinner had disappeared with astounding speed, and even the deep-dish apple pie was being slivered into oblivion.

"Unusually so for this time of year. We need a good, soaking rain. Just so lightning doesn't set something on fire before it comes. I can't remember when I've seen it this dry this early."

"Any trouble with people not taking care of their campfires?"

Katelyn shot Luke a suspicious glance. Had there been more trouble with the campers he'd encountered?

"Not really. Most people respect the land. Crazy thing, though. I came across a fellow today emptying his ashtray onto the ground at one of the lookouts. There was still a live ash in one of the butts. Can't imagine what he was thinking about." Ben shook his head, perplexed.

"Green and white camper, California plates?" Luke probed, sitting slightly straighter in his chair.

"Yes. An older model, mid-seventies. Tall fellow with a wife and at least two children."

"He's the same one who came after me when I told him to douse his fire more thoroughly. I'll be glad when his vacation is over and he has to go home. I hope he's more careful with his own property."

Ben nodded. "I know where they're camping. I've thought about driving out to check on them. I don't trust that fellow. He got too angry when I talked to him—belligerent."

Luke nodded in agreement. "Same thing happened to me. If only he'd realize what a prairie fire does in dry grass. We could lose miles of land to one match."

Katelyn shivered in the warm air. She'd seen a fire in the Badlands once, raging like an inferno. The sparse population of this area had gathered to fight it, like ants beating against the turn of the tide. Two men had died that night, engulfed in a fire that burned around behind them, building its own perfect trap. Prairie fire was nothing to be tampered with.

"More dessert, Luke?" Mary inquired.

"No, thanks. I'd better not. I'm supposed to be at the musical soon...." His refusal was punctuated by the insistent chime of the telephone. Ben scraped his chair backward against the kitchen floor to answer it. As his hand fell across the receiver, the strident scream of Medora's fire whistle called its meager volunteer army to duty.

The men's eyes met across the table-top. Katelyn heard the sharp intake of Luke's breath and the grating yelp of her father's voice as he answered the phone.

"Ryan here. Yes. No. Stanton is here, too. Yes. Right away." Ben dropped the phone into the waiting cradle. "Well, Luke, looks like the worst has happened. There's a fire at the edge of the park. It started near a campground. The Dickinson fire department has been called. We'd better get out there."

"Daddy..."

"You stay here with your mother, Katelyn. Luke and I will be back when we can."

The clipped, expressionless order dismayed Katelyn, and she dropped the hand she had extended to her father. He had no time to allay her rising fear.

Luke encircled her limp fingers with his own for a brief moment. She could feel the dry heat of his palm and the rough, irregular contours of calluses on his work-hardened hands. Many a leather rein and hemp rope had traveled through those hands. But as they comforted her, they were as light as eiderdown and as tender as the flutter of a butterfly's wings.

Katelyn's eyes sought his. "Luke?"

"It may be a while, Katelyn. It depends on the fire's path and the wind."

"It's not too far from town. We've got to get going." Ben ran his eyes across his wife's face and his daughter's. "Now."

Luke applied a gentle pressure to the tender hollow of Katelyn's palm. "See you later." He followed Ben through the screen door, and the two women stood motionless as the Jeep sprang to life in the driveway. Only the distant and fast-disappearing drone of the

92

motor told them the men were gone.

"Let's get these dishes done, Katelyn. No use letting them sit around." Mary slapped the palms of her hands against her gingham apron.

"Mother! How can you think of doing dishes now?"

"We've got to be busy, child. That fire could burn all night. It will do no good to be idle. Put the salad away. It will go bad sitting out in this heat." Mary secured the knot of her apron and whisked a stack of plates to the sink as Katelyn stood staring at her mother's rigid back.

Bravery in the face of adversity. Mary Ryan had had more than her share of experience. Katelyn's grandfather had died in a burning building in Williston, crushed under the weight of a fire-weakened roof, still holding the last member of his young family. Mary knew what a holocaust a single flame could generate. And Katelyn knew it, too.

"There. That's better. I just hate to leave a dirty kitchen." Mrs. Ryan dried her hands on the rim of her apron. "Now we can go."

"Go? Where are we going?" Katelyn traced a pattern across her upper lip and under her jawbone with a damp towel. The night was getting warmer and warmer, as though nature's thermostat had gone awry.

"Uptown. Someone will know if they've gotten that fire under control. And I think I'll burst if I don't get out and walk. Your father's too old for this sort of excitement—and so am I." Mary pushed the screen door open and marched into the night.

If her father was too old for this, Luke was too young. Too young to die. Too young to be swallowed in the flames that threatened them all. Fear lodged in Katelyn's throat. Only now did she realize how important Luke had become to her in these brief, idyllic days. Only now, when he could be precipitously snatched away, she realized his importance.

"There you are! Have you heard the latest?" Arne and Jean were standing in the crowd gathered outside the saloon. Tourists and residents were milling about, speculating on the fire. "The wind has shifted, and the fire is burning right into the path of an oil rig. They've called for bulldozers, plows, and anything that can dig up dirt. They need a firebreak wide enough to protect that rig—or everybody and everything around it will go up in flames."

The oil rigs! They dotted the countryside at the perimeters of the park like prehistoric monsters dipping their noses into the earth to drink. They plumbed liquid gold beneath the surface day and night, becoming as much a part of the landscape as the farms and ranches that were scattered around the countryside.

"Where will they get the equipment, Arne?"

"Most of the oil companies have a bulldozer or two. Dickinson has some, and so does the county. The farmers are pulling in plows. Jean and I were just going to drive down the highway to see the fire from the road. Want to come?"

Mary's eyes revealed a glimmer of fear. "Not me, Arne. I've seen enough fires to last me a lifetime. But Katelyn can go if she wants to."

"Coming?"

Nodding silently, Katelyn followed them to their pickup truck. As they wound upward out of Medora, she riveted her eyes to the road, scanning the black horizon for the orange glow that meant destruction.

"There it is." Arne pulled to the side of the road. Far ahead a brightly burning bonfire was cheerfully licking the night sky with dancing tongues. From a distance, it was a cozy, benign sight.

Katelyn scrambled from the pickup and into the box of the truck for a better view. The wind on the bluff whipped her hair into a frenzy of wild curls. Idly she wiped a stray strand from the corner of her lip.

Luke was out there. And her father. She could see miniscule dots moving at the base of the flames. Bull-dozers. Men. The flames leaned over the figures like the threatening crest of a wave, about to break over them, engulf them. Headlights were playing on the oil rig. The flames inched closer even as she watched.

"Arne, will they get out of the way if they can't pro-tect the rig?"

"I hope so. But there are some fighting fools out there."

Her father. And Luke. They'd never give up. They loved the animals, the land, too much. They'd fight the destructive fire until there was no fight left.

Katelyn felt suddenly ill. Beads of perspiration broke on her body, and the forceful wind cooled her skin until she shivered with chill. The conflagration raged below them—beautiful, vicious, deadly.

"Well, if they use their heads, they'll get that fire-break built and get out of there," Arne reasoned.

"And if it jumps the break?" Jean's voice carried weakly through the night.

"An act of God, I'd say. And nobody should tamper with an act of God."

God.

He'd been cropping up a lot lately. Katelyn had spent twenty-six years without Him and suddenly He was everywhere. Disrupting her peace of mind. Toy-ing with her emotions. Tampering with her spirit. God and Luke Stanton had been doing all that.

But what good is God if Luke and Daddy die?

Luke would have an answer to that, but Katelyn

couldn't think of one. God would have taken them away, that's all. A dirty-dealing deity, that's what He was. Giving her Luke and then whisking him away.

But Luke wasn't dead. And neither was her father. The fire was playing tricks with her mind, convincing her that neither would return. Maybe God would give them back to her—give her another chance.

Another chance. Luke *was* her second chance. He was her opportunity to wipe Randy from her life, to replace him with a good and honest man, a *whole* man—morally, spiritually, emotionally. That was why the terror of losing him raged so deeply and painfully within her.

Luke was like new life in spring, a shoot of hopeful green sprouting from a dead landscape. And all of that new hope for her life was out there in the blackness, silhouetted against a flaming sky.

Katelyn railed against her helplessness. If Luke were here, he would pray. Katelyn wasn't even sure *how* to pray. Luke could have taught her. But Luke was gone—maybe forever.

Chapter Seven

"We've got to go back to town, Katelyn." Arne shook her with surprising roughness. Katelyn flinched. How long had he been speaking to her?

"Sorry, Arne. Have you been talking to me?"

"We can't stay any longer, kitten. Maybe they'll have some word in town on how the firebreak is working."

Nodding dumbly, she crawled into the cab of the vehicle. Her limbs felt wooden and her skin clammy. Self-discovery on a breezy hilltop did nothing for one's physical condition. She had been buffeted both internally and externally by searing, high-powered winds.

The crowd had grown. Street lamps brought into sharp relief a sea of tense faces. Katelyn found her mother on a bench, her hands folded quietly in her lap.

"Mom?"

"Someone has been hurt, Katelyn. They don't know who. An ambulance just left for Dickinson."

"Badly?" The word lodged in her throat and came out in a breathy whisper.

"Apparently. Something to do with one of the bulldozers. It's dark out there but for the lights and the fire. One misstep and…" Mary's voice trailed away in a sob.

"Daddy?"

"No one knows. They're in such a hurry to finish the firebreak they've become careless. Maybe we should be thankful only one has been hurt—so far."

Katelyn wanted to put her fist in the air and rail at Luke's useless God. If He was so almighty, then why didn't he do something? Send rain. Snow. Sleet. Fire engines.

Fire engines? At that moment fire engines were winding their way down the side streets into Medora!

A cheer rose at the far end of the street and rippled its way through the crowd like the undulating motion of someone shaking a blanket—the wave of noise crescendoed until it broke over the street with a loud snap. The returning engines were a sign that the firebreak had held!

"Go home everyone! Go home! Your men will be coming shortly." Someone on a bullhorn blared instructions into the street. Katelyn and Mary turned obediently toward the Ryan residence. The men would come home.

Just then the grating whine of an ambulance shattered the celebration in the street. The red globe cut into the night, spraying the buildings with an eerie red glow. Then the siren wound down to a whimper and the bloody gash of light dimmed. The driver opened the window and stuck his head through the metal frame.

"If no one else needs me here, can I go home?"

A nervous bubble of laughter broke over the crowd.

"Go! Go! Be glad we don't need you!"

Katelyn turned a wavery smile toward her mother. Tears spilled across Mary's cheeks.

"Mother! What's wrong?" Thoughts of the first ambulance, the one that had left with its injured passenger, barrelled into Katelyn's brain. "Did you hear something about Daddy?"

"No, honey, it was Eddie Taylor that was hurt. Someone just came to get Irene."

Katelyn felt a mingling of sorrow and relief. Ed Taylor was her father's dearest friend. But her father and Luke were safe.

"We'd better get home. Your father will be there soon."

And where will Luke go? To the big tub in the little cabin, no doubt. Away from her, just when she needed to talk to him. Then she remembered the Jeep. Perhaps he'd bring her father home and she could see him, if only for a moment. She wanted proof positive that he was safe and still in one piece.

Luke and Ben were already on the doorstep when Mary and Katelyn arrived.

"Ben!" Katelyn's mother threw herself headlong into her husband's arms. Making clucking, consoling noises, he led his wife into the house.

Katelyn found herself staring wordlessly into Luke's soot-smeared face. All the frenzy she'd experienced on the hilltop lost momentum as she stared at the tousled mop of dark hair. Finally his mouth opened in a bright smile, his teeth gleaming even whiter in contrast to his dark moustache and the dusty powder of grit covering him.

"I'd like a greeting like that, too, if you don't mind."

A moan, half relief, half joy, escaped her lips, and she flung herself about Luke's neck, oblivious of the charred powder the front of Luke's shirt ground into the pale green sundress. Her mouth sought the smoky tartness of his lips. Her eyes burned from the singed smell of his clothes and from the tears summouned by his kiss.

She was hungry for the sooty arms about her and the burnt flavor of his mouth. Then she felt him begin to chuckle against her lips. His chest rose and fell in laughter against her.

"So that's what it takes to get you into my arms." He held her away from himself and ran his eyes across her features. "At least one good thing came out of this disaster."

"Luke, don't tease me. I was frightened—very frightened."

"For your father?"

"And you." She hung her head, eyes studying the pebbles at her feet. "There were so many things I didn't get to tell you, things to explain—and to ask about."

"And tonight you thought you might never get another chance?"

She nodded dumbly. Now that he was safe, it seemed a ridiculous notion. But he appeared to understand. He, more than anyone, deserved an explanation. She wanted to give him the definition, to draw him the picture, of who Katelyn Ryan was. Tell him why she was so wary of men. Let him know how she'd come to care for him. Ask the questions she had about his God. She'd almost lost the chance to share these things with him. And whether Luke wanted to hear them or not, she would not jeopardize her opportunity again.

Tears trickled from beneath her lowered lids. Luke

pulled his blue bandana from his pocket to wipe them away. But before he touched the cloth to her cheek, he gave a low chuckle.

"I don't think this will help." He waved the blackened kerchief under her nose. "Do you want to come to the cabin while I clean up? Then I can wipe those tears and smudges away with something that won't leave more dirt than it picks up."

Her heart fluttered in her chest as she nodded. She needed him tonight. Perhaps he needed her as well.

"What about your folks?"

She smiled. "They'll never notice I'm missing. And if they do, I think they can figure out where I went. Or at least who I'm with."

Nodding agreeably, he boosted her into the Jeep. Field dirt and soot puffed into the air and settled again on her skirt. She'd be dirtier than Luke before the night was out. And she didn't care a whit.

"Here we are." He pulled the Jeep to within inches of the porch steps. Even Gus lifted his head to see what the excitement was about. His tail pattered twice on the board porch before he drifted to sleep again.

Luke began peeling off his shirt before he entered the house.

"Would you go in and run some bath water, Katelyn? I'm going to try to shake off some of this grime out here." As he shook the shirt over the railing, motes of dust floated up into the porchlight.

"Sure. Do you use bubble bath? A rubber ducky?"

He grinned. "I want to get clean tonight, so I will forego my flotilla of unsinkable rubber boats. Locate a towel and washcloth, if you don't mind. And holler when it's ready."

On her way to the bathroom, Katelyn noticed he'd

come a long way on the cabin. The fireplace looked complete and the piles of scrap wood and stones had disappeared.

She hummed as she adjusted the water temperature in the big tub. She felt very domestic. Luke was a meticulous housekeeper. She found a stack of terry towels in navy and white folded neatly in the linen closet. Everything about Luke was simple and unpretentious, but earnest. He was a good steward.

Katelyn surprised herself with the biblical-sounding thought. Luke inspired such vagaries.

She stepped back onto the porch to announce, "The tub's as full as I could make it." Her eyes widened at the unwittingly sensuous display before her.

Luke's bare back gleamed in the porchlight, in spite of the fine sifting of soot that had worked its way through the fibers of his shirt. He'd tossed his boots and socks aside and was barefoot and beltless. As he bent over to scratch a fat tabby behind the ears, the muscles of his back rippled with reserved strength, each well-defined sinew flexing in the pale light.

Then he picked up one of the ever-present kittens and stood, his toe lightly grazing old Gus's side. The dog shivered amicably in his sleep and buried his nose even deeper between his paws. Luke allowed the kitten to curl, purring, against his silken chest. And then he smiled.

He was beautiful. Like a revered statue cut of marble, his body was finely chiseled and delineated. Strong. Supple. Sensuous. Katelyn's breath caught in her throat. She was glad for the shadows on the porch, for a blush was rising to her cheeks and descending to her toes.

"I like being waited on. It's a new experience.

102

Thank you." He dropped the kitten and brushed past her on the way to the bathroom. Katelyn followed him with her eyes.

What was happening to her anyway? She was intoxicated with the sight of him, the sound of him. He was like no other man she had ever met. But it went deeper than that, beyond the physical. He was so...kind. She had a sneaking suspicion that the qualities she questioned were the same ones that drew her to him.

The Christianity business was probably what made him so compassionate and undemanding. It drew her to him and it drove her away. She drew a deep sigh. They would have to talk. She would be honest with him, lay bare her secrets. She was tired of concealing from her family what she had suffered at Randy's hands. If her secrets drove him away, so be it.

She desired for herself the peace and self-acceptance Luke had. She'd come home to heal her wounds. Perhaps Luke Stanton was the balm she needed.

"That's much better." He strolled onto the porch, still toweling his damp head. His skin was three shades lighter with the soot gone. The golden honey glow was back. He'd pulled on clean jeans and a white V-necked T-shirt.

"Now I'm the dirty one." She brushed ruefully at the skirt of her sundress.

"Well, at least you can get the smudges off your face." He took the corner of his damp towel and began to wipe away the grime she'd collected kissing him. She breathed deeply, savoring the smell of fresh soap and Luke on the towel.

He paused, towel midair, to smile at her. "Well, I guess this evening had a happy ending, after all."

Katelyn swallowed. Hard. The emotions and the

memories of the night engulfed her. Fear—of losing those men most important to her. Love—for her father. Confusion—over Luke's faith. Hatred—Randy's legacy. A tear slid from beneath her silky lashes.

"But maybe I was wrong," he continued, "or you wouldn't be crying."

She flung her head backward until she could feel the tendrils of her hair skimming beneath her shoulder blades and gave a gusty sigh.

"Crying, laughing, screaming, I don't know what to do!"

"Don't move. Hold that thought. I'll be right back." He touched his index finger to the tip of her nose before disappearing into the cabin. Momentarily he returned, lugging a foam pad and a brightly woven Indian blanket. He flipped the blanket around the foam and moved to the heavy, raw-wood porch swing at the darkened edge of the stoop.

The swing shuddered and swayed as he nestled the padding into the seat. He patted it twice with the palm of his hand before spinning around to face her.

"Now, then. It seems to me we're going to have a conversation long enough to warrant sitting down. On padded seats. Come cry, laugh, or scream over here— with me."

He held out his arms and she stumbled into them. Her arms slid along the cool cottony shirt on his chest. He led her to the swaying swing, and they dropped into it, their bodies never separating. She burrowed her nose into his shoulder, and the aroma of soap and skin drifted about her.

"Luke, you're so...good to me!" The accusation was punctuated by a wail, and tears began to stream down her face in earnest.

She felt him start in surprise.

"You make it sound as though I should apologize, Katelyn! Would you like me to be belligerent for a while?" His amused drawl floated on the night air. He set the swing rocking with his right foot. His left was curled under him.

Where to begin? How to tell him of the vow she'd made after Randy's deception? What to say of the emotions that raged within her tonight, as incendiary and volatile as the prairie fire?

"Is it raining on my shoulder, or do you need my handkerchief? I have a clean one now."

She gave him a watery smile. "You think I'm crazy, don't you? Crying like a baby for no apparent reason."

"No," he said softly, chewing on his bottom lip. "We carry a lot inside us, Katelyn. Sometimes a crisis brings it to the surface. You were very frightened this evening—for your father."

"And for you."

"Glad to hear it." His even teeth flashed briefly in the moonlight. "But there's more. I've known that since I met you."

There in the soothing lullaby motion of the handmade swing, Katelyn poured out her heart to a man who really listened.

"I was engaged to be married, Luke. To a man I met in Chicago. We were to be married this summer. We hadn't known each other very long. I was lonely in Chicago, and he was charming. And he seemed to need me. I know those weren't reasons enough to fall in love, but I felt so out of place in the city that I clung to him like a lifeline. And he didn't seem to mind."

"What happened, Katelyn?"

A crackle of bitter laughter escaped her. "He *needed*

me all right. He courted me by night and embezzled funds from his company by day. I was a simple country girl from North Dakota, a veneer of respectability, the perfect cover."

"I'm so sorry." Luke's eyes darkened to muddy pools. He was running his thumb up and down the tender cord of her neck. The unconscious pressure he applied revealed the strength of his emotion.

"Not as sorry as I was. He planned to marry me, Luke, but not because he loved me—not even a little. He didn't even give up the woman he was colluding with on the embezzlement scheme." The pressure Luke was applying to her neck became painful.

Suddenly he seemed to notice the pain he might be inflicting. He pulled his hand away and flexed it against the back of the swing.

"How did you find out?"

She laughed scornfully. "His attorney called after the arrest. I was trying on my wedding gown at the time." Ironically she parodied, "Congratulations, many happy returns, your husband-to-be is a thief.

"I was a number-one, first-class fool, Luke. Looking back, I can't even imagine how I agreed to marry a man I scarcely knew. We'd only dated a few months. It never would have happened if I hadn't been so homesick for the Badlands."

He grasped her shoulder and began to knead the soft flesh between his fingers, silently pleading for her to relax.

"Do your parents know?"

"No. No one does. No one but you."

"Thank you."

"What?" She peered at him.

"Thank you. For trusting me."

106

A chortle of disdainful laughter rose within her. "Trust. That's the key word, isn't it? I vowed I'd never trust another man again." She jumped from the swing and began to pace the porch. Kittens scattered under her feet. "And here I am, pouring my heart out to a man I've known only a few days. No wonder I was such as easy mark for Randy! I'm a fool, pure and simple. A fool!"

All her pent-up anger and hatred and resentment came crackling to the surface. Her thin veneer of invincibility crumbled. All the sublimated hurts and fears flowed from her, hot lava tears from the volcano of her emotions.

"Katelyn. Come here." Luke had not moved from the swing. He was motionless except for his eyes following her across the floor. He seemed unafraid of the torrent spilling from her.

Caught between the poles of her emotions, Katelyn vacillated between the warm security of Luke's command and escape into the black night. If she stayed, she'd be giving in again, reneging on her vow. If she left, she'd be alone.

Tonight, loneliness seemed too much to face. She melted onto the swing bonelessly.

Luke's eyes probed gently, but his hands never moved. One still rested on the back of the swing; the other clenched and unclenched against his thigh. He shivered imperceptibly as tendrils of her red hair grazed his forearm.

Katelyn could sense the control he was exercising to keep from touching her, his unspoken promise not to use her for his own design.

"I'm so confused." The words broke forth as a sigh, and she allowed her head to drop back against the porch swing and Luke's bare arm. The silence was broken only by the creaking of the swing and the occasional mewling of a kitten.

"I'm not like your former fiancé, you know."

Katelyn opened her eyes to study his features in the dim light. "Aren't you? You're a man."

"There are all kinds of men, Katelyn. You had the misfortune to attach yourself to an unscrupulous one."

She sighed. "Sometimes I think a lack of scruples is an integral part of a man's nature, Luke, whether he wants it to be or not."

If she expected him to protest, she was disappointed, for he nodded thoughtfully, agreeing. "That's true. We're all sinful by nature. But that's only the beginning of the story."

Her curiosity piqued by his odd answer, she straightened to study his eyes. Luke's eyes could spin a story without words.

He shifted slightly, his arm grazing her shoulders, and she found herself sinking into the inviting crook at his elbow.

"I don't understand you, Luke. You're certainly unusually willing to admit to a corrupt nature." She smiled, softening the tone of her words.

" 'For all have sinned and fall short of the glory of God,' " he quoted, watching her.

Katelyn jumped. Not this religious mumbo jumbo again! Though she tried to pull away, Luke was ready for her, his arm trapping her about the shoulders.

"I don't like it, Luke. I don't like this kind of talk. It just confuses me. And anyway, what does it have to do with you and me?"

"You just said mankind was corrupt. I agreed. But we do have another option, a way out, so to speak. We can be forgiven and start living as our Creator would have us do. It's not so difficult to understand, Katelyn. Try."

"And you're saying that this God of yours is what makes you different?"

"I suppose so."

"Forgive me, Luke, but believing that will take some time."

"Time?"

"The true test of anything—a man, love, anything— is time. If this God is as influential in your life as you say He is, then time will prove that. Right?" She looked to Luke for affirmation. "If He sticks by you and you stick by Him in the bad times as well as the good, well, maybe then I'll begin to believe in Him."

"I can accept that, Katelyn. It shows you've already learned from your mistakes."

"You're not angry with me?"

"No. In fact," and he gave her a blazing smile, "I kind of like it."

"Why?" She pulled away suspiciously, but he drew her back again.

"Time. If I have to withstand your test of time, that means you'll be around to observe me until I've passed whatever test you've created for me. I like that, Katelyn, the idea of spending lots of time with you."

His index finger traced a pattern across her features, meandering on to her lips. Then he met those lips with his own, gently tickling her warm, pliant mouth. She saw him grin as he captured her willing kiss, and she felt the low chuckle in his belly. When he raised his head, his eyes were shining. He spoke so softly she wondered for a moment if she had imagined it.

"Yes, sir, Katelyn, I think this is going to be a mighty

fine summer." They rocked silently together on the big swing to the symphony of an unoiled hinge.

Free of the resentful emotions she'd harbored so long, Katelyn's head began to nod and bob against Luke's shoulder. She smiled slightly as she felt him slip his arm beneath her knees and brace her back with the other. He carried her, curled against him, to the Jeep.

She yawned sleepily as they pulled into the driveway in front of her home, waving away his offer to carry her to the house. Luke might risk the impropriety of carrying her, sleeping, into her parents' house, but not that of allowing her to spend the night curled into his front porch swing. He'd passed one brief test of time.

Chapter Eight

Luke was at the kitchen table drinking coffee when Katelyn, stretching broadly, meandered into the kitchen.

"Sleep well?"

Her eyes flew open at the sight of the visitor. He and Ben were polishing off a plate of doughnuts and a pot of coffee. Mary kneaded her husband's shoulder through the crisp ranger's uniform, last night's holocaust obviously not forgotten.

"I must have. I didn't even hear you talking in here." Katelyn filled her mug and speared a doughnut with her index finger. At least she hadn't scared Luke away with her incoherent babblings. Even so, the fire had loosened her tongue a bit too much.

"Luke came to tell me that Eddie Taylor isn't hurt as badly as we first suspected. Last night we thought his leg was crushed by that dozer, but apparently it's just broken in two places. Clean breaks, at that."

Ben shook his head. "Funny thing about the location of that fire...well, never mind."

"Tourists?" Luke finished for him. Everyone knew of the belligerent traveler both he and Ben had confronted.

"Maybe. Most likely a cigarette butt somebody didn't grind out. But the fire started outside the park. No camping ground nearby either. The only thing right there is oil wells."

"Maybe there was a spark from some equipment," Luke offered.

"I just don't know. I have a funny feeling about something, but I can't put my finger on it. It's not the fire, really. It's those trucks that went by. They weren't familiar to me. Oh, well." Ben stood and grinned. "I won't figure it out sitting here getting fat. I'd better get to work. What's on your schedule for today, Luke?"

"Same as usual. But I thought maybe Katelyn would like to join me after the chateau closes. I'm going to a rodeo in Dickinson. I have to pick up a horse I purchased, and I thought she might like to ride along."

Ben whooped, "Brave man! Asking for a date in front of her parents! What if I protested?" He slapped Luke hard across the shoulder.

"You're too wise for that, Ben. It's your daughter's answer I'm worried about."

Katelyn gave the two a disgusted look. "I'm so glad I have a say in this matter. I'd love to turn you down and put you both in your place, but I don't want to. I'd be delighted to ride along, Luke."

"Great. See you later." He swung out of the chair and toward the kitchen door. Katelyn waved at his retreating back.

"I like that boy," Ben commented, throwing back the last dregs of his now-cold coffee. Mary followed him to the door, and Katelyn was left in the kitchen, alone for her introspection.

I like him, too. But only time would tell. Maybe even Luke wasn't all he seemed.

On her way to the chateau she stopped at her

father's office. She could hear a one-sided telephone conversation drifting into the hall as she neared the door. Purposely she slowed her step. Her father hated to be interrupted when he was on the phone.

She listened, waiting for the conversation to end.

"Did you notice any unusual traffic around the fire last night?...Oil trucks, tankers? How many?...That's what I counted, too....Do you know of any good reason for them to be there just then?...Uh-huh....Okay. I'll keep an eye on it. Somebody around here must know something."

The phone fell back into the receiver as Katelyn walked into her father's office. She was surprised by the black look grazing his features.

"Problems, Daddy?"

"I hope not. But something strange is happening and I need an explanation."

The look on her father's face frightened her. The normally placid planes were tense with concern. Whatever the phone call had been about, it was important.

"Well, I just wanted to say hi," she stammered. "I'm leaving with Luke from the chateau and bringing my clothes along so..."

"Luke? Did you say Luke?" Her father's tone brought her up short.

"Of course, Luke. Remember, at breakfast he..."

"Oh, of course." Ben wiped a hand across his eyes. "Have fun then. We can talk about this tonight."

Summarily dismissed, she wandered back to the street. What was the "this" to be discussed later? What *had* that telephone conversation been about?

"Ready?"

Katelyn started at the sound of Luke's voice. Her

113

father's troubled mutterings of this morning still nagged at her. Whatever he'd heard on the telephone must have smacked of trouble. But now was not the time to worry about her father. She scrambled from the cross-legged pose she'd taken on the chateau's porch.

"I suppose. What do you think?" She pirouetted with arms outspread, displaying slim, stone-washed jeans and a violet Western shirt.

Luke plumped out his cheeks and exhaled in a low, breathy whistle. His eyes danced with a merriment Katelyn could only hope she had put there. "I think we'll pick up the horses and come home. I don't want to be guilty of starting any stampedes among the cowboys."

Gratified, she smiled to herself. She felt downright coquettish this evening. With a man who looked like Luke to escort her, any woman would. She discreetly eyed him from below the rim of her hat.

He pushed his summer straw hat back on his head, propped one booted foot against the porch, and began to study her openly. His dark eyes traveled across her face until they trapped her own.

"Well?"

She swallowed hard, fearing she would choke on the sensations he had aroused in her. Luke was able to elicit strange responses to the most innocuous statements.

"Well, what?" she finally stammered, suddenly feeling out of her league. No man had ever left her tongue-tied before.

"Well, are you ready to go to pick up my horse? We'd better get going. I didn't plan to stay long at the rodeo. Funny thing, but I didn't get much sleep last night." He looked at her sharply, amusement and something else playing in his eyes.

Yearning to know what he was thinking, hoping his sleeplessness had, in some small part, been due to thoughts of her, she nodded. "Let's go." She stepped across the porch to meet him and found herself extending a hand toward him. If he wasn't going to make the first move, she would. Holding hands was harmless enough.

But as his fingers touched hers and a pulse of excitement bolted its way through her arm to a queasy point at the base of her stomach, she began to wonder if anything was harmless when it was done with Luke Stanton.

They were mostly silent on the ride into Dickinson. Luke drove leisurely, unmindful that nearly every car on the road passed them by. His rig had surprised Katelyn, who had expected the rough and dusty little Jeep to be waiting for them below the hill. Instead there were a big ivory and chocolate brown pickup and a horse trailer with the name of the stables emblazoned across the side. Now he rested his right arm against the back of the seat, idly watching the nose of the trailer through his rearview mirror and rubbing his right thumb against the crest of Katelyn's shoulder.

Relaxed, she gave in to her urge to curl her head down and rest her ear on the top of Luke's hand as it made a circular path across her shoulder.

"Ummmmmm." A blissful sigh escaped her.

"Most definitely."

"What?" She raised her head and questioned him with her eyes.

"I was agreeing with that nice little sound you made. I'm sorry I made you straighten up like a fence post. Come over a little closer and relax again."

She hoisted herself across the gap between them and settled in next to Luke. The seam of her jeans grated against the thick denim line of his. Her shoulder fit like a most proper puzzle piece just under his arm, and he dropped his wrist over her shoulder.

"That's better."

She thought so, too, but she wasn't about to say it. She'd fallen too quickly under the spell of this man, and she needed to bide her time. *The test of time.* If Luke withstood that, then she'd let him know her feelings.

"So how were things at the chateau today?"

"Bitsy tripped and fell against the table in the dining room. We almost lost the Minton china. The whole table rattled and clanged, but luckily nothing broke. She shook for an hour afterward. Poor thing."

"It always seemed to me they used too many dishes anyway. What do you need besides a plate, a fork, and a mug?"

"You'd be no good in fine company, Luke. Medora de Mores had three cups for every person. One for coffee, one for tea, and one for the demitasse. And, of course, two saucers."

"Do I dare ask what the second one was for?"

"One for the cup and one to pour the coffee into. Then you could blow on it to cool it." Although she tried to keep the lecturing tone in her voice, the idea of blowing into a saucer of coffee had always struck her as funny.

Luke chuckled, the laughter surfacing from deep within.

"Now don't make fun. You and the de Mores have something very special in common." She couldn't keep the teasing from her voice, but he agreeably took the bait.

"All right. What do we have in common, Miss Know-It-All?"

116

"They had the first indoor bath in the Dakota Territory. And I'd venture to say you have the first sunken tub in the city limits. So there!"

He tilted his head to one side. "You might be right. Haven't taken a poll of the bathtubs in Medora lately. What other bits of interesting information do you have for me?"

"Nothing. You have to buy a ticket to get more. I'm supposed to tantalize you with scraps of interesting history and lure you into taking the tour. Have I succeeded?" She turned to smile and found her face very near his. His foot was almost entirely off the gas pedal, and they were coasting down the highway.

"In tantalizing me? I'd say so. In fact, I'm beginning to wonder if we should bother to pick up that horse at all...." He was about to steer to the shoulder of the road and roll to a stop when she tapped the top of his boot with her own.

"Oh, no, you don't. You promised me a ride into Dickinson and I want to *get* there." Beneath her playful facade crept a seed of fear. Things were moving too quickly. She felt a surge of gratitude when he nodded evenly and accelerated the vehicle. He was patient. *Another test of time.*

"This must be the place." Luke pulled up into a throng of expensive pickups and horse trailers similar to his own. Dust swirled about, never settling before tires, boots, or hooves stirred it again.

He swung out of the cab and held both arms to Katelyn. He lifted her to the ground as though she were air and turned back to the cab for a sheaf of papers resting on the dashboard.

Katelyn studied him from behind as he reached into the high-mounted truck. He was a lean blue line. As his shirt pulled tightly across his back, Katelyn could see

117

every graceful curve of his spine that separated the solid muscles rippling under the shirt. His slim waist as it disappeared into the rich, tooled-leather belt was nothing but sleek, firm muscle.

Katelyn absorbed it all in seconds and managed to compose herself as Luke backed out of the pickup cab with his papers in hand.

"Come on. These papers entitle me to one handsome stallion who's going to please every mare in my pasture." He grinned impishly beneath the dark moustache and moved toward the middle of the melee.

He missed Katelyn's raised eyebrow. *A lady pleaser, huh? This horse might just turn out to be a lot like Luke himself.*

She had to run to catch up with Luke's rangy gait. Then his pace slowed as he neared a trailer with a lustrous black stallion tethered near it. A low, admiring whistle slipped from between Luke's teeth.

"He's really a beaut, isn't he?" Luke stood with his thumbs hooked into the leather circle of his belt, admiring the horse.

The black beast whinnied and pawed, jerking impatiently at the leather and rope holding him fast. His coat reflected the waning daylight like black glass. The muscles of his body shivered in anticipation of a long run, and the black coat shimmered along his spine like the moon on black waters.

"Hello, Stanton. Come to pick up your purchase?" A round face appeared around the edge of the trailer.

"Yup. Looks like he's all groomed and ready to go."

Now a round body followed the moonish face. Katelyn nipped at the inner corner of her lip to keep from laughing. The man looked like a series of balloons strung together and dressed in Western garb. Even his stubby calves were narrow at the knee and ankle, thick

118

and round in the center. Little pockets of fat marked each joint of his fingers.

"You got a good buy, Stanton. Caught me at a weak moment, I must admit. Surprised me, too. Normally when cowboys come to barter, they don't have enough cash in their pockets to pay for a pony ride, much less the whole horse. No sir, I believe I sold this fellow too cheap." The pudgy, over-eager fingers danced across the horse's neck.

Katelyn watched with interest as Luke tentatively examined the animal. Then, without warning, a disturbing thought occurred to her.

Where did Luke get all the money to buy an animal like that? Jake Pelton hadn't made much from the stables. In winter the horses ate a good deal of the summer's profit. Luke's prices were higher and his business more brisk, but it took a heap of change to buy an animal like this one. And to build a cabin of such quiet luxury.

But an eager question broke into her reverie. "What do you think of him, Katelyn? Think the mares will like him?"

"If I had four legs and an appetite for oats and prairie grass, I'd think he was wonderful." Katelyn laughed and edged closer to the creature. "In fact, I do anyway. What are you going to call him?"

"The name's Ben Butler. Got labeled as a baby for his contrary ways." Katelyn had almost forgotten the round little man until he spoke.

"Don't you remember that story, Katelyn? Ben Butler was the horse that had the nerve to rear under Theodore Roosevelt, fall backward, and pin him to the ground. Broke the point of TR's shoulder." Luke's caressing hands never left Ben's coat.

Familiar as she was with Medora's history, she'd

119

never sought out the tales spun around Roosevelt's horses. "Well, the horse didn't do it on purpose, surely."

"Didn't he? Old Ben supposedly did it twice in a row. When Roosevelt's friend Sylvane Ferris tried to mount him, he backed up and did the same trick again. But I'd wager this fellow is from a nicer-natured mold."

The cranky Ben Butler's namesake was nuzzling into Luke's hip pocket. Katelyn had seen Luke reach into that particular pocket and produce sugar cubes for the trail horses. Luke crooned while the big animal searched the pocket for a treat.

"That's it, big boy. You know what you want." Then Luke's whispered caresses were swept away in an eddy of swirling air.

Katelyn felt an empty pit in her midsection. She was jealous of the horse! The innocent creature could accept Luke's attention unquestioningly. If she would accept it, the gentleness he afforded the animals wouldn't be lost on her.

"Let's take Ben to my trailer and then see what's happening in the arena." Luke was suddenly next to her ear.

"Fine." Katelyn nodded abruptly and matched his pace as they wound their way to the trailer.

"Want to watch the calf roping for a while?" he inquired, drawing her back to the present—and to himself. Her eyes slowly cleared.

"Calf roping? Brrrrr." Katelyn shivered in the warm air. "I don't like seeing that poor young thing yanked off its feet and slammed to the ground. I'm always afraid its neck will be broken."

"Then you must hate broncobusting and bull riding."

"No, not at all. I find that exciting."

"If you can't stand to see a calf roped, how can you watch a man get bounced around on the back of a bucking critter and stomped into the ground if he doesn't run fast enough when he's tossed off?"

"The men ask for it, Luke. The calves don't. The men make the choice to ride. They have to accept the risks." Katelyn stared somberly at him, her eyes alight with indignation. "Poor calves. They have no choice."

"I'll thank you to quit talking about this, Miss Ryan. You've singlehandedly ruined all the pleasure I've ever taken in rodeoing. I never wanted to break my own neck riding a bull, but I suppose I didn't worry too much about anyone else's." Luke had her sternly by the shoulders. His voice was serious, but his eyes were laughing.

"I'm sorry. You didn't tell me you traveled a rodeo circuit."

"Hardly that. But I enter a few for the fun of it." Luke pointed toward an open space on the fence enclosing the arena. "If you can stand a couple more calf ropings, the bull riding is coming up next."

He hoisted her to a perch on the fence. Katelyn caught her breath and held it as Luke's hands went about her waist. Only when he released her and swung himself onto the fence beside her did she expel the breath. Her lungs were about to burst, but she preferred the pain to the sensation of Luke's touch.

As Luke's eyes focused intently on the action at the middle of the arena, Katelyn's inspected him. He was, as usual, in soft, much-washed denim. His boots were dusty, the leather scraped and peeling. He wore no jewelry except for a heavy silver ring with a turquoise stone.

Katelyn's eyes paused on the ring. Exquisite. The sil-

121

ver gleamed with a rich warm patina. The central darkened hollow of the intricate filigree held a vibrant blue-green stone. That ring was quite likely valuable.

Randy had worn a ring. Once he'd raised his hand in anger to her. All she could remember was the cold, hard eye of the stone.

"Hang on, Porter! Hang on!" Luke was yelling so loudly that Katelyn started from her reverie.

The calf roping had given way to bull riding. Katelyn watched the spine-snapping ride with her eyes half closed. Surely the only reason Porter endured the whiplashing atop the bull was to avoid the churning hooves at the other end of its body. The angry creature leapt and turned in a vain attempt to shake the irritating weight from its back.

With a particularly violent jerk, Porter's Stetson hat sailed under the bull's hooves, reminding Katelyn of a perverse Mexican hat dance as the beast hooked upward and landed, flattening the crown into the dusty earth.

Cowboys. Men with guts, a horse, and a rope. And the love of a simple, uncluttered land. Katelyn studied Luke from the corner of her eye.

Entranced by the contest in progress, he leaned forward on the fence, gripping the slivered rail for support. His eyes followed every arch and spin of the bull, lighting with appreciation as if he were witnessing a finely choreographed ballet.

And perhaps it is. Nature's ballet. Man and beast. This was a country where one faced his problems head on and rode them through. Katelyn's eyes traveled to the arena just as a catcher pulled Porter from the bull's back. The excited clapping about her signalled a successful ride, and Luke's hand on her arm pulled her back into the present.

"Somehow I get the feeling you're not in the mood for this tonight."

"Maybe not. I'm sorry. My mind seems to be as hard to tame as that bull out there. But don't let me ruin your fun."

"Not likely. Want to leave?"

Curtly, she nodded. For some odd reason, Luke's ring, the bull ride, everything evoked melancholy whispers of the past. Katelyn found herself growing short and edgy. Her skin crawled with unspoken tension.

Her father's odd tone on the telephone had set the mood for the day. Innocently, Luke had stepped into the disquiet.

His fingers encircled her elbow, nudging her toward the edge of the unruly crowd. The warmth of his fingertips reached through the fabric of Katelyn's shirt, and irritably she shook him away.

"I can find my way by myself, thank you." Head high, shoulders square, she stomped away through the crowd until it closed about her, engulfing her in a sea of Stetsons and rough denim. She glanced back to see if Luke was following her but felt a wave of disappointment when she saw him embroiled in conversation with a seedy-looking man. She didn't care. He could talk all night if he wanted to.

She found her way back to the trailer and planted herself forlornly on the running board of the pickup, her knees doubled up against her shoulders and her fingers wound tightly in her hair, the palms of her hands clamped to her head.

"Hello."

She raised her eyes to meet Luke's. "Hi."

"I'm sorry."

"For what?"

"For whatever made you stomp off like that. I've got a lot of faults, but making pretty history buffs mad usually isn't one of them." He hunkered down beside her, spreading his knees wide and resting his elbows on them.

With his eyes even with hers and his breath so near she could almost feel it graze her cheek, the past began to give way to the present in Katelyn's mind. Luke's real, warm-bodied presence could help her, if she'd let it happen.

"I wasn't angry with you."

"Could have fooled me."

"I just started thinking about...things."

"Chicago things?"

She nodded unhappily. "Every time I think I've put that all behind me, something crops up to remind me. Tonight it was your ring."

"My ring?" Luke stared at his right hand in surprise. "Did your ex-fiancé have a ring like this one?"

"No. His was just a ring, a diamond set in platinum. Showy and expensive. He tried to hit me once, and all I can remember is that ring flashing in the light. I remember thinking that anything that pretty shouldn't hurt me."

"He hit you?" Luke spit the words out from between clenched teeth. His hands knotted and flexed unconsciously.

"No, but he started to. He caught himself in time. Before the week was out he'd been arrested. Apparently he knew he was suspected and had a nasty case of nerves." Katelyn projected her lower lip and blew aside a stray lock of hair that had tumbled over her forehead.

Then a smile lit her eyes, beginning as a pinpoint of light deep in the hazel depths and brightening until a warm steady beam shone from her features. "I'm more trouble than Ben Butler, Luke. You'd keep a skittish pony in line. Don't do any less for me."

The even white line of Luke's smile brightened his face; and he reached to wipe the errant forelock from her eyes. His fingers washed across her gently, like a lick of night wind.

"Then come on, you unbroken filly, you. Let's get old Ben into the trailer and take him back to Medora. Any more gloomy nonsense from you, and you'll have to ride with him instead of me."

"That warning should keep me in line," Katelyn acquiesced, suddenly feeling much, much better about herself and the evening.

Ben was more than willing to take up residence in the roomy horse trailer. He'd poked his nose through the gratings before Luke and Katelyn settled themselves inside the cab of the truck. Luke eased out of the congested parking lot and onto the highway.

The radio spun out a twangy country tune, and wind from the open windows disheveled their hair. Luke drove with his left arm resting on the open window frame, three fingers guiding the steering wheel. Katelyn settled her head into the curve of his other arm and edged her knee closer to his.

Farm and ranch lights dotted the horizon, and stars speckled the sky like white drops on a dark paint cloth. The land spoke of far-reaching, unbroken plains, vast and lonely. But Katelyn knew of the rugged terrain lurking ahead of them.

"Melancholy monotony." Luke's voice drifted to her on a breath of cool wind.

"What did you say?" Katelyn felt helpless to move from the cozy cocoon of his arm, drifting as she was on the sea of darkness and the scent of him. All she

could see of him were the planes and peaks of his profile. Somehow, the vision was mesmerizing.

"Melancholy monotony. That's how Roosevelt described the plains. Once you drive out of the Badlands, there's boundless prairie. At the peak of one
gently rolling hill, all you see is another in the distance, like a succession of ocean waves."

"You're very poetic, Luke Stanton." Katelyn
squirmed out of his arm to stare at him.

"That's Roosevelt speaking, not me. I just like it,
that's all. It's like God dropped a surprise in the middle
of nothing, just so those first pioneers would have a
change of scenery. First the prairie, then the patch-
work, then the serrated bluffs. No one could take the
land for granted after that."

"Are you giving God or the Little Missouri credit for
carving the Badlands?" A hint of derision sneaked into
her voice. The ride had been so peaceful until Luke
brought up God.

"They worked together on this one, Katelyn. Part-
ners in a grand construction project still under way."

"Seems to me God must have stepped out of the
partnership," she responded dryly. "I haven't seen any
signs of Him lately."

"Maybe, but I doubt it." Luke was grinning broadly
now. She'd stiffened back into a little fence post, just
as she always did when religion cropped up in the
conversation.

He dropped the subject and began kneading her
rigid shoulder. Momentarily the tension left her, and
she sank against the seat, close to him.

Katelyn closed her eyes and focused on the rumbling wheels beneath her. The steady vibrating of the
pickup grew ragged as Luke turned from the highway
onto the gravel road to Medora.

126

When the pickup shivered to a halt, Katelyn opened her eyes to the porchlight of her own front door.

"Home already?"

"I think you fell asleep partway here. At least you were very quiet." Luke tucked her closer under his arm and explored the tendrils of her hair with light, observing fingers.

"I haven't felt so relaxed in ages," Katelyn admitted truthfully. The night had purged her of some of the ill feelings she'd harbored so long. Luke's undemanding presence drew the poisons from her system like a warm, healing poultice.

A dull chuckle filled the cab. "I haven't felt like this in ages, but I'm not relaxed." Luke edged her around to face him, taking her face between his hands and drawing it closer to his own.

The streetlamp behind her was reflected in his eyes, so they sparked with blue, fluorescent light. He unconsciously licked his lower lip with the tip of his tongue before he smiled and lowered his lips to her own.

Katelyn was engulfed in a sweet, warm flood of emotion. Hungrily she sought to taste those tenderly searching lips, responding more eagerly than she had thought possible. Luke pulled her to him until she could feel the rise and fall of his chest and the sharp edge of his belt buckle.

As she squirmed away from the offending buckle, Luke released her. She could read the concern in his eyes.

"I'm sorry Katelyn. Was I moving too fast? I know there are some ghosts of the past still haunting you..."

"No ghosts tonight, Luke. Just an aversion to being poked in the stomach with your belt buckle." She tapped the buckled with a pretty, polished nail.

127

Relief washed across his features like a cleansing rain, but he didn't attempt to take her in his arms again. Instead he pulled forcefully on the door handle and slid to the ground, holding his arms open to catch her. As Katelyn slid after, disappointment welled up inside her.

"Maybe we should be glad that buckle came between us, Katelyn. I see your father glaring out the kitchen window. I don't want him out here chasing me off his property with a shotgun. He's a sharpshooter if I ever met one. He could take the heels off my boots with me in them. How about one proper goodnight kiss?"

Muffling a giggle and keeping one eye on her father in the kitchen window, she obliged. Arching her neck in anticipation of his kiss, she threw her arms about him, tangling her finger in the soft strands at the base of his neck.

Rather than bend to meet her, Luke wound his arms about her waist and lifted her. As their lips met for a searing, crushing moment, they both heard the clang of a dropped kettle within the Ryan house.

Katelyn could feel Luke's gusty chuckle against her lips as he set her down on the hard-packed earth of the driveway.

"That sounds like a hint."

"I thought Daddy was beyond that sort of thing." She kicked the dirt in disgust and no little amount of disappointment, for Luke was obviously making ready to leave.

"Katelyn, if I ever had a daughter as lovely as you, I'd ride shotgun on every date."

"And leave the child's mother home alone to worry about the two of you?"

"Well," Luke paused meaningfully, "that would depend on the mother, wouldn't it? I imagine it would be within her power to entice me to stay home."

The kettle dropped again before Katelyn had the opportunity to respond. Throwing her arms wide into the air, she turned toward the house.

"I surrender, Daddy! I'll come in!" Then she paused and turned back to Luke. "Thanks...for everything."

"You're welcome. Can I see you again?"

"It will be hard not to."

"Good."

She smiled at the satisfaction in his voice. Blowing him a playful kiss, she turned away. As she drifted dreamily into the kitchen, she heard the engine come to life and the rig pull from the driveway.

Rubbing a cautious hand over her kiss-swollen lips, she meandered into the kitchen. She needed to remind her father she was a big girl now. It was no longer necessary to frighten off ardent admirers—at least not this one.

But the playful thoughts were erased from Katelyn's mind by the troubled expression on Ben Ryan's face. Worry lines furrowed his brow, deeply creasing the normally placid countenance.

The question broke from Katelyn in a breath of fear. "Daddy, what's wrong?"

Chapter Nine

Ben's ruddy complexion was mottled, splotches of red bleeding onto his neck. His fingers wandered nervously over the handle of the cast-iron frying pan he held. A mist of nervous sweat glazed his features. Katelyn had never seen her father look so distraught.

A dart of fear lanced through her. "Is it mother? Is she all right?"

"Your mother is fine. She's sleeping. I couldn't share the pleasure, so I thought I'd come out and fry myself a few eggs. But I can't seem to keep from dropping this unwieldy pan on my foot."

Katelyn took the pan from her father's unnaturally loose grasp. "I'll fry the eggs. You tell me what's wrong." Efficiently she settled the pan on the stove and reached into the refrigerator for the eggs.

"Wrong? Nothing's wrong." Ben's voice was flat with disguised emotion.

Katelyn shattered the second egg against the rim of the pan. The sticky white and yellow gel oozed between her fingers.

"Don't lie to me, Daddy. You look terrible. Something is troubling you and you might as well tell me. You'd better get it off your chest before you break every toe on both feet." She stirred the eggs briskly, shattered yolk and all, into some semblance of an omelette. Her mind was far from her cooking.

Instead of answering her question, Ben Ryan asked one of his own. "Did you have a nice evening with Luke?"

"Of course I did. He's very sweet, Daddy. But what does that have to do with why you're so shaken tonight?"

Katelyn was startled by her father's odd answer.

"I don't know if it has anything to do with it, Katelyn. I wish I did." His voice drifted off musing. "I wish I did."

"Daddy?" A leaden weight was settling in Katelyn's stomach.

Ben sighed deeply and stretched an arm about his daughter. "I suppose I should explain, although nothing makes any sense to me either. It all started with that phone call this morning."

Katelyn pushed the eggs away from the heated burner and followed her father to the kitchen table. When they were settled across from one another, Ben began to speak.

"Something funny is going on in the park."

The questions in Katelyn's eyes encouraged him.

"You know the park is rich with oil." Katelyn nodded. That was only logical. Productive drilling rigs circled the park perimeter on privately owned farm land.

"The oil companies are restricted to drilling on private lands. That's why you never see a rig within the park itself."

She nodded again. Her father seemed intent on unwinding his story like a ball of yarn, slowly at first, then more quickly as he got to the heart.

"Have you ever heard of 'slant drilling,' Katelyn?"

131

She shook her head blankly. Another oil term, she supposed. Oil workers used as much jargon as cowboys and doctors and every profession bent on keeping their knowledge top-secret.

"It's a term for a particular type of drilling. It's also called directional drilling because they dig a deviated hole. Occasionally there is an underground reservoir within an oil field that extends beneath inconvenient places to drill. If the field stretches under a town, like Gainsborough in Lincolnshire, England, or under the sea as it does at Huntington Beach in California, a curved hole is dug so the reservoir can be tapped without vertical drilling. Slant drilling has been used as far as a mile or two out under the sea. It replaces the need for those big offshore oil rigs that pump off our coasts. Instead, they drill from the shore, deep into the ground under the water at an angle. That places the bottom of the well under the inaccessible surface location. The pump can remain on dry ground and still siphon oil from a good distance out at sea."

"Seems sensible," Katelyn acknowledged, still unsure what all of this had to do with herself and her father—or Luke.

"We suspect there is some slant drilling going on right here, Katelyn. We've come to believe there is a rig or two next to the park, illegally siphoning oil from beneath national lands. If it's being done, it's a clever form of thievery."

"But those oil wells are dug and maintained by reputable companies, Dad. I can't believe that something like this could happen."

"We have no argument with those operations, but a new, independent oil company began drilling here a few months back. If they've got a line into the park, they could drain off enough oil from one rig to make

132

more than one millionaire."

"What first made you suspicious, Dad?"

"The trucks that move around that well. I've spied tankers sneaking away from there in the night. That's just not common practice. If they are pumping it out of the park, they don't want anyone to notice those late-night trucks."

"What does this have to do with the telephone call you received this morning? Or with Luke?"

"There were tankers sighted near the fire, trying to slip away, I suppose. And one of the fellows working on this talked to your friend Luke earlier in the day."

Her friend Luke? Hadn't he been her father's as well? What had changed Luke's status so quickly?

"I think you'd better explain." The brittleness of her voice surprised her. She sensed she was about to hear something she wouldn't like.

"Alfenson, the fellow I'm working with, spent some time out at the stables chewing the rag with Luke. Luke's been seen with a member of the crew on more than one occasion, and Alfenson wanted to find out casually if he'd dropped any hints that the setup wasn't completely aboveboard."

"So?" That hardly seemed enough to point a finger toward Luke.

"Alfenson thought Stanton gave some pretty evasive answers, Katelyn. Maybe he didn't know anything and was being completely honest, but still, Alfenson thinks Luke's hiding something."

"He *thinks* Luke is hiding something? Is that enough to hang a man? On what another man *thinks*?" Katelyn's voice pitched nervously. She didn't want to hear this, not tonight.

"Stay calm, honey. It's probably nothing. Luke's been here longer than the new oil company, and far as

I can see, he's been downright—well—religious. But he has put a lot of money into the stables lately, new riding stock, the cabin. Makes you wonder how much he makes with the animal resource department. Poor old Jake never made more than a living wage when he had the stables. Course, Jake was the world's poorest manager, too. Maybe Stanton just knows how to make good use of what he gets."

Katelyn's mind drifted over what she knew of Luke's finances. The big sunken tub, the costly silver ring, the gleaming black stallion. Maybe he did have more money than his simple lifestyle suggested. But could all that talk about God be a cover for underhanded dealings? Or was it sincere belief? The possibilities tore through Katelyn's mind like racing winds.

She wouldn't believe these things of Luke. She couldn't. Or could she? Luke would have to be proven guiltless. Then she could relax in the assurance that her experience with Randy was a one-time hurt.

Then the telephone rang. Its strident clamor broke into the silent house like a midnight intruder—unwelcome, unwanted. Ben picked up the receiver.

"Ryan here…. Oh, hello, Alfenson. What do you know?"

Katelyn stared at the phone, willing good news to spring from it. But when he finally lowered the receiver to its cradle, Ben was grim.

"Luke was seen in Dickinson tonight, talking to the same oil man that he's been seen with before. Did you two separate anytime, Katelyn? Did he have a chance to meet anyone without you?"

"No, of course not, except…."

"Except what? You'd better tell me."

She shrugged, the words sticking in her throat like insects on flypaper. "I *did* see Luke talking to someone, but he couldn't have taken more than five minutes, Dad. That's not enough time to plot and scheme!"

"Nevertheless, it was enough time to meet the driver of one of those tankers. I don't like it, Katelyn. I'm afraid Luke knows something he's not telling us. And the longer he delays, the guiltier he's going to look."

"Aren't you placing blame rather quickly, Dad? Luke could have a million reasons for talking to those drivers."

"I know, and only one is a bad one." Ben shook his head tiredly, "Maybe we're chasing shadows. Maybe Luke *couldn't* answer Alfenson's questions. I don't want him involved in his. He's too nice a guy. But until we get it settled, he's under suspicion. Maybe he'll explain himself to you Katelyn."

Or make a slip and give himself away. Aloud she inquired, "You mean, you want me to spy on him?"

Ben's eyes grew sad and dim. "I'm sorry, Katelyn. When it's over, if Luke is cleared, I'll be the first to apologize."

He turned to leave the room, his shoulders stooped under the weight of unproven suspicions and betrayed loyalties. Trust was a rare commodity growing ever more scarce. Katelyn stretched out a hand to call her father, but dropped it to her side in profound weariness herself as she slumped into a stiff-back kitchen chair. As the initial numbness eased from her body, a rush of tears stained her cheeks.

Not Luke too! Wasn't there an honest man anywhere? Only when the grandfather clock in the hall spilled out the hour, did she rise and stumble toward her room.

At the threshold, Katelyn righted herself, squaring

her shoulders and thrusting her delicate chin into the air. She had made a decision. She would give Luke time. She would not judge him prematurely.

This would be a test for God, too. If Luke could lie so glibly, then the Creator he espoused couldn't amount to much. But if Luke was sincere...well, maybe even she would give that God of Luke's a chance. A dry laugh rattled in her chest. Luke had no idea how much responsibility was riding on his shoulders. Could he and the God who supported him handle it?

Subdued and weary, Katelyn stretched out on her bed in darkness. Morning would bring new light and more challenges to face.

It hadn't been a dream. The nightmarish conversation of last evening was real after all. Katelyn roused herself unwillingly. Given half a chance she would have "taken to her couch" like a delicate Victorian lady. Instead, like the hardy contemporary female she was, Katelyn swung her bare toes to the hardwood floor and reached for the skimpy underwear strewn across the bedpost.

She longed to slide into a pair of cotton shorts and a cool skin-skimming T-shirt. The high-necked, floor-length dresses she wore at the chateau became more burdensome with each degree the thermostat crawled upward. Rain had to come soon. The spring greenery had shriveled and the countryside showed its winter colors. What the land needed was a paintbrush of summer rain to sweep along the hills and intensify their bright colors.

Still in a cotton wrapper, postponing the moment when she would zipper herself into the petticoats and lace, Katelyn padded to the kitchen. Her father was at the table. But much to her relief, so was Bitsy.

"Good morning! What are you doing here?" Katelyn stifled a yawn and curled herself into a stiff-backed chair.

"My husband needed the car today and didn't know what to do about getting me to work. The Jeep has a flat tire, and I'm not up to riding a horse into town. I didn't think you'd mind if I came here and rode to the chateau with you."

"Not a bit. But it's early yet, isn't it? We don't open for a couple more hours."

"He needed to get on the road. I thought maybe I could talk you into breakfast uptown. What do you say?" Bitsy's eyes sparkled with enthusiasm. Everything was an adventure for her. Even the mundane came to life under Bitsy's enthusiastic consideration.

"I'd love to. We can stop back here to dress before work. I've hardly been downtown since the chateau opened." Pleased with the diversion, Katelyn swung into action. She and Bitsy were on their way before Ben had the chance to remind her of their late-night conversation. Katelyn needed time to think that conversation through, a day away from her father—and from Luke.

Trudging toward the center of town, Katelyn ruefully watched her long, golden legs become powdered with a fine smattering of dust. Then she glanced about her, still charmed by every part of the little village snuggled beneath the towering buttes in the Little Missouri valley.

"I was reading some wonderful old newspapers last night," Bitsy volunteered, "some clippings my husband's grandmother had saved in a scrapbook. They were written nearly fifty years ago and already lamenting the changes in Medora."

"Changes? I can't think of a place that stays more the same!"

"The writer was lamenting the disappearance of rowdy cowboys who used to shoot up the town every Saturday night. Said there hadn't been a first-class murder here in years—as if that were a curse instead of a blessing!"

"It must have been quite a place. Just think, Bitsy—the nearest sheriff was a hundred-fifty miles away. A drunken cowboy could cause quite a bit of mischief and still escape to the hills by the time anyone got around to looking for him."

"Bill Jones," Bitsy proclaimed, then clamped her lips together as if that name summed up the entire conversation.

Katelyn nodded, smiling. She remembered that name from her own trek through Medora's past. Bill had been a playful hooligan who orchestrated scenarios for railroad travelers on their way west. When the train stopped in front of the old Pyramid Park Hotel, its passengers were treated to a round of gunfire and falling bodies outside their windows. After they'd witnessed what appeared to be a good deal of violent bloodshed, the train would pull away and the "corpses" would scramble to their feet and head for the nearest saloon for a drink and a good laugh.

It was no wonder the cowboys were boisterous, Katelyn thought. Anyone who drank saloon alcohol diluted with river water, colored with chewing tobacco, and seasoned with a dollop of red pepper would have to do something to burn off the internal fire.

She and Bitsy turned into the cafe just as Arne and Jean were leaving.

"Hello. Fortifying yourselves for another long, hot

afternoon?" Arne already appeared to be melting. He dabbed vainly at his forehead with a handkerchief.

"I heard rain is predicted for tonight or tomorrow," Bitsy volunteered.

Katelyn found her mind drifting away from the idle small talk of the others. No matter how she tried to occupy her mind, Luke crept back into her thoughts. All day Katelyn battled the thought of him, his tender, deferential manner and his patience.

As she mouthed the tour narrative through the mansion, her mind hung tenaciously to other thoughts. *He can't be involved in the slant drilling! Not Luke! Please, not Luke!*

By evening Katelyn was exhausted. Mentally wrestling with the possibilities left her drained and bewildered. But this time she was in control. If Luke was not what he seemed, at least she'd had fair warning. She was not at the mercy of events this time.

Her father had confided in her. And though he'd exacted her promise not to say a word about the illegal drilling, he'd not asked her to avoid Luke.

As she and Bitsy closed the chateau for another day, an idea came to Katelyn. Perhaps *she* could exonerate Luke in the eyes of her father. And she desperately needed to know in order to save some shred of her own self-esteem—that she'd come to value, to love, an honest and decent man this time. The only one who could prove that to her was Luke himself.

As dusk approached, Katelyn made her way to the little cabin nestled in the hills. The air was a hot blanket wrapped about Katelyn's legs as she walked toward the stables. Her crisp, brief khaki shorts and cotton blouse wilted, and the fabric limply brushed against her sun-darkened skin.

But the weather was changing. A dark wall of sky

loomed to the west. The heavenly tent over Medora was collapsing quickly as stormy clouds rolled in. Occasionally a whiff of damp, cool air wound itself about Katelyn's legs. The fingers of the storm tickled her senses. She shivered and increased her pace.

A soft, warm light was glowing in the window of the cabin. Gus and the kittens, more sensitive to weather changes than humans, were clustered at the base of the steps. Gus was gnawing hungrily on the few wisps of green grass in the mostly shady corner between the porch and the first raised tread.

A sure sign of rain, Katelyn thought to herself. Perhaps it was an old wives' tale, but she'd watched the animals and it was true. Their behavior predicted a weather change far more surely than a TV forecast.

Gus took time from his chewing to wag his tail in greeting. The kittens tangled en masse about her ankles as she tried to mount the step. Picking up the one with the loudest rumbling purr, Katelyn threaded her way through the throng to stand at Luke's door. Suddenly shy and unsure of her plan, she paused, fist poised midair, ready to knock.

"Come on in!" Luke's voice carried through the rough wood door. He must have seen her approach. Nervously, clutching the kitten much too tightly and making it mewl in complaint, she turned the knob and stepped inside.

"Well, hello." Luke had not risen from his seat. Katelyn's eyes widened in amazement as they traveled about the room. The last time she'd been here the room had been little more than a rough shell. Tonight it was a home.

The bookshelves were stained and filled. Hundreds of volumes marched in precise rows across floor-to-ceiling shelves. Western art in rugged barn-wood

140

frames glowed from beneath strategic track lights. A woven Indian rug in muted grays and rust spread its way into all but the farthest reaches of the room. And a fire burned brightly in the fieldstone fireplace. Two guns, mounted over the mantel, gleamed dully in the soft light.

Luke sat with his back to the fire in a pillowy chair, his long legs propped on a soft ottoman, a book open across his lap and, most surprising of all, a pair of tortoiseshell glasses in his hand.

"How do you like it?" He uncrossed his legs and began to stand up.

"It's wonderful! Like a picture out of some Western rancher magazine! How did you manage it since I was here last?"

His low chuckle reached her and set up a disturbing stirring in the pit of her stomach. Everything this man did affected her.

"It wasn't so difficult, really. I had the shelves built. All I had to do was stain and fill them. Then I could unroll the rug and hang the pictures. I *did* own some furniture, you know. We Western cowboys aren't completely uncivilized. It's been a few years since we've had to live out of a saddlebag." Luke smiled and stuck the bows of the glasses into his hair, propping them high on his head. Suddenly he looked more like a scholar than a cowboy.

"You'd better let go of that kitten before you squash it."

Katelyn dropped the poor creature, and it scampered to safety under the second easy chair.

Words escaped her. She stood tongue-tied in the middle of his living room. Luke was like a prism, giving off a different light each time she looked at him. He was multifaceted, intriguing, mysterious.

Finally something struck her. The jarring discrepancy she'd first sensed became tangible. "Luke, you've got a fire in your fireplace! It must be a hundred degrees outside!"

He had the grace to look sheepish. As he waved her into the chair across from him, he explained, "I turned on the air conditioning."

Then he laughed aloud at the dumbfounded expression on Katelyn's face. "If you haven't noticed already, we're in for a storm before the night's out. The temperature is going to drop in a hurry. I decided to anticipate the change and be ready for it. As soon as it starts to rain, I'll turn the air conditioning off. I just finished putting the last of my books on the shelves, and the room looked like it needed a fire to cozy it up."

He was right. It made the room perfect.

"Coffee?" Luke was waiting for an answer.

"Oh, sure. If it's made, that is."

"Always. Cream or sugar?"

"Black." It occurred to Katelyn that she and Luke knew very little about each other—even how they took their coffee. Yet their relationship seemed timeless—to be measured in eons rather than minutes or weeks.

As he swung out of the big chair and walked to the kitchen, she furtively leaned over to see what he had been reading.

A Bible. She should have guessed. And open on the lamp table at his side was a book of poetry—epic poetry. His glasses lay across the page so she couldn't make out more, but she had seen enough. Surely this man couldn't be involved in the nefarious dealings of a shady oil company! Surely not!

"Hungry?"

He was back. Instead of the battered tin coffeepot

she'd somehow expected, Luke was carrying a slim copper carafe and two ceramic mugs. He settled his load on the small table and poured a cup of steaming black brew.

"I said, are you hungry?"

Katelyn smiled impishly, some of her equilibrium finally returning. "Do you cook?"

"On occasion. Beef stew tonight. Want some?"

Hunger pangs had been nibbling at her insides all afternoon. Food had seemed too much bother until right now. Suddenly she was starving.

"All right. If you don't mind company for supper."

"I'm glad for it. I always fix a lot, and then I don't cook again until the leftovers are gone. I'd appreciate having one less day of warmed-over stew. Sit still. I'll get it."

She watched his back disappear into the kitchen. The rough cowboy garb and the stylish, preppy glasses would have seemed incongruous on anyone but Luke. But he wore life well—in any form. Before she could speculate further, he was back with two steaming bowls of stew with thick, hard rolls perched on top and spoons angling out of the bowls.

"Sorry I don't have a table yet, but I thought I'd build one this winter when things get quiet. Don't spill it in your lap. It's hot."

The beefy broth sent up wisps of savory steam. Katelyn inhaled the meaty perfume with eyes closed tight.

"Smells wonderful."

"Wait till you taste it. That's the test." Luke rested the ankle of his boot across his other knee and settled his hips more deeply into the big chair, but he did not begin to eat.

Katelyn, suddenly reminded that she was the guest

and he the host, held her bowl before her waiting for him to begin.

"Will you mind if I say grace, Katelyn?"

She nearly dropped the steaming plate into her lap, but she nodded. What else was there to do?

As Luke dropped his chin against his chest and closed his eyes, she studied him. This was his God, not hers. She didn't feel the necessity to show *that* much reverence.

"Dear Heavenly Father, thank you for this food and this new and special friendship. May it thrive and flourish with Your blessing. Thy will be done, Father. Amen."

Katelyn's heart trembled at the words. Was Luke asking a blessing on their friendship? That their relationship might thrive and flourish—if God approved it? Didn't she and Luke have some say in the matter? More baffled than ever by what compelled him, Katelyn dug her spoon deep into the rich broth in her bowl. Some tangles were not easily untwined. Luke was one such tangle.

"Wonderful!" The exclamation escaped from Katelyn's full mouth.

"Thanks. Glad you like it."

"Do you use a recipe?"

Luke threw back his head and laughed. "I don't mind flattery, Katelyn, but this is the first time anyone has *ever* asked *me* for a recipe!"

"No flattery. I've just never met a man before who is a better cook than I am."

"If you really want to know, I used carrots, chunks of beef, some celery and an onion, a few tomatoes, the rest of the stuff I cooked last week and couldn't bear to eat another night...."

"All right, all right! So you're a creative cook! You

144

fascinate me, Luke Stanton."

She regretted the words as soon as she said them. They caused Luke to set down his bowl and study her. His dark, penetrating eyes X-rayed her soul.

In a desperate bid to change the subject before he could respond, Katelyn pointed to the open book on the table.

"I see you like poetry."

Obligingly, Luke took the bait. "It's a recent passion. Teddy Roosevelt liked epic poetry, and I decided to see why. The grandness of it appeals to me."

Each twist of intellect and tenderness charmed her more completely. And with each moment the spectre of Luke involved with the illegal drilling rigs loomed more blackly.

She desperately wanted Luke to be free and innocent of her father's suspicions. She could imagine him more easily on his knees, bowed in prayer, than in cahoots with low-life oil pirates.

Much to her chagrin she found herself loving this man, despite the shadows that still hung over him. If she were hurt again, she wouldn't survive it.

Chapter Ten

"Katelyn? Are you still with me?"

She sprang back to the present with a jerk. She'd drifted so far from Luke's voice that it took the sound of snapping fingers to return her consciousness to his living room.

He was hunkered down in front of her, balancing on the balls of his feet, his forearms resting on the length of his thighs. His jeans stretched tightly, freeing the back of his shirt from his belt. His coffee mug dangled carelessly from his fingertip, and his free hand moved back to wrap itself around the bowl of the mug as he studied her intently over its rim.

"Katelyn? What are you thinking about?"

For once, recklessly, Katelyn allowed her mouth to flip into gear before her brain, and the question of the evening popped out.

"Luke, what are you about, anyway? What's important to you? What motivates you, makes you tick?"

He laughed softly and rolled back on his heels and stood. "I'm not sure you're ready to go into that with me, Katelyn."

Buoyed by her boldness, she persisted. "And what do you mean by that?"

"You're like a little wet hen every time the topic of religion comes up. Are you sure you want to get into that this evening?"

"Yes, I am."

Somehow it didn't seem so distasteful tonight. He'd aroused her curiosity, no doubt about that. How a man's man like Luke Stanton could so easily admit to being vulnerable was intriguing, and she felt more open to persuasion tonight here in the cozy cabin. She curled into the chair, unconscious of the defiant thrust of her chin.

Luke sat down too, leaned back into his chair, and stretched his legs. The bottom of his boot grazed Katelyn's leg.

"I'm a very lucky man, Katelyn, to be living here, doing what I am. I have to be grateful to God for that."

"But you're well-educated, bright, resourceful. You'd be living where you wanted even if God didn't have any part in your life!"

"But I feel I'm living within God's will here. It's where He wants me to be."

"Tending horses?" That hardly seemed a divine calling.

"Partially. But you forget about my work with the animal resource people. It brings me a good deal of pleasure to ensure that the creatures here can flourish in their natural environment. It's good for them and it's good for us humans as well. We *need* places to visit and see how it was before man came through. We need to be reminded that there's another life outside of office buildings and freeways and shopping malls."

"I suppose that's true. But would the environment really change so radically here if it were left alone?" Perhaps she'd never appreciated enough the sight of a deer and its timid fawn or the playful scurryings of the prairie dogs.

"Establishing the West upset the balance of the environment so that between sixty and seventy million buffalo in the early 1800s dwindled to fewer than three hundred by the turn of the century. That's one animal, Katelyn, and a big one. Even the most careless of humans would notice its dwindling numbers. The smaller animals might not be so lucky." Luke stretched his palms across his thighs in a massaging motion. "It's stewardship, making wise decisions and investments with the gifts you've been given. I'm a steward of God's earth, Katelyn. And I like it. If you're going to accept me, you've got to accept that as well."

Stewardship. If that's how Luke felt, surely he wouldn't be caught up in a slant drilling scheme. Though she had no more proof than before, she felt oddly comforted. He hadn't disappointed her.

"Thank you."

He glanced at her, startled. "For what?"

"For sharing that with me."

Luke's eyes suddenly looked old and wise beyond his years. "Do *you* have something that you want to say to *me*?"

For a moment, panic spread through her. Did he know about her father's suspicions? Then she realized he was talking about Randy. Distractedly she threw her head against the chair.

"Do I? I don't know. The more I try to put my experience in Chicago behind me, the more often it crops up in my thoughts. Sometimes I think it's going to drive me mad. I keep wondering how I could have been such a fool."

"You were lonesome," Luke offered.

She nodded wearily. "Terribly. I grew up in a mite of

148

a town where everyone knew my name and even what I had for breakfast. Chicago was a real culture shock. I must have clung to Randy like a drowning woman clings to a life preserver. I'd filled my head with the notion that the city would hand me friends on a platter."

"And instead?"

"Instead I got a handsome, smooth-talking con man who needed a respectable cover."

"He couldn't have been so bad, Katelyn, or you never would have been attracted to him."

She shot him a grateful glance for that. "Randy wasn't bad. In fact, he was considered quite a catch by my acquaintances at work. He was successful and charming and…intriguing."

"Intriguing?"

Katelyn laughed ruefully. "A carry-over from a severe teenage case of marquis-fever. I thought any man I married should have a bit of intrigue about him—to keep things interesting. I know better now. I tried to force Randy into the mold of my expectations instead of seeing him as he really was. I could have saved myself some pain if I hadn't done that."

"Sometimes we have to learn the hard way."

Katelyn looked across at him. He'd put on the glasses that made him look so scholarly—and vulnerable. Sunk into his chair, he braced himself with his arms flat against the armrests. She had the urge to move toward him and curl herself against the broad wall of his chest. Luke Stanton might allow himself to be vulnerable, but he was still strong.

A puckish light began to gleam in his eyes. He crooked his index finger to her, inviting her into the tempting curve of the arms she'd been admiring.

Slowly she uncurled her legs and settled her toes

against the floor. With a surge of disappointment, she watched him unfold from his chair and stand.

"Air conditioning."

It took her a moment to understand him.

"I'm going to turn off the air conditioning. In case you haven't noticed, it's started to rain."

When he returned from the thermostat, instead of sinking into the chair again, he held his arms out to her. Hesitantly, then with more enthusiasm, she moved toward him. Her last steps were taken in such haste, she tumbled into his waiting arms.

Resting her head against his chest she could hear the steady throbbing of his heart and feel each predictable rise and fall of his chest. Whether from the heat of the fire or some internal heat, Katelyn felt herself grow warm.

Luke swept an arm under her knees and carried her to his chair, arranging her on his lap as easily as he would one of the kittens. And she snuggled to his chest, content for the moment to listen to his heart and the early patterings of Medora's first summer rain.

As the blaze weakened and faded in the firebox, so did Katelyn's resolve. Luke's fingers wound their way through her hair, gently twisting and tugging the fire-bright curls. With his arms about her, she felt secure, but when he shifted his weight and the arms fell away for a brief moment, reality crept into her mind again.

She had fallen in love with Luke Staton.

It was the very thing she had vowed to avoid. Worse yet, her father had posed questions about him she could not answer. Nebulous suspicions ate away at her. And to heap confusion upon confusion, Luke himself had assaulted her little remaining peace of mind with his talk about God.

He'd opened that one closed and resolved area of

her mind to new examination. Her father had never said he believed in God. So she hadn't either. Until now. Now she wondered about God's existence. If Luke believed Him to be real, well, maybe there was a remote possibility He was. Even under the cloud of suspicion the slant drilling had fostered, Ben Ryan had more than a grudging admiration for Luke.

Thoughts swirled like eddies of fast-moving air as Katelyn lay stone still against Luke's chest. The comforting movement of his hand in her hair and the sharp-soft feel of his chin resting against the top of her head warred with the unwelcome doubts.

Her gratitude to him was exceedingly great. Even holding her, he did not press her beyond what she was willing to give. He seemed content with her presence against his body and unafraid of their silence.

But she began to feel the knotting tension deep in her belly. The doubts were taking hold. An unexplainable sadness swept over her. If only she knew the truth about Luke! Then she could allow herself to love him. *If only!*

She broke away from him with a wrenching sigh. She could see the sadness of her face reflected in his own.

"Katelyn?" The twining fingers seemed hesitant to leave the tangled nest of her hair, but she felt him smooth her flame-bright locks and drop his hand to the armrest.

"I think I should be leaving, Luke."

"Already?" She felt a nudge of pleasure at the disappointment in his tone.

"I've eaten your food and wasted your time. You should be glad to get back to your...books." She eyed the Bible on the table.

Luke's perceptive glance followed her own. The

151

source of her present discomfort was obvious.

"You've also made my evening a very pleasant one. I hope I've returned the favor." He made no mention of her apparent questions—or doubts.

She turned, her face resting very near his own, and sighed. "Have you? I don't know. You mix me up, Luke. I can't understand you."

"I thought I was fairly simple and straightforward." The smile in his voice also lit his eyes.

Simple and straightforward? Hardly. He was as complex and bewildering as the hills in which he lived. Of a million strands of color and depth, nature had woven in his personality intriguing shadings of light and shadow as beautiful as the hills.

Who and what was the real man? The unassuming trail guide? The horseman? The believer? The well-educated scholar? The accomplice in the slant drilling scam?

She felt torn in a psychological tug of war between her budding emotions for Luke and the creeping, insidious mistrust from her father's questions. She had to get away, think, to sort out the questions—to find the answers.

She laid a hand on Luke's wrist. The warmth of his skin sprang to her fingers, and as her hand encircled that warmth, the pulsebeat throbbed in time with the beat of her own heart.

With a freshet of renewed determination, Katelyn murmured, "Straightforward? I hope so. Good-bye, Luke."

And before he could stop her, could offer to return her to her father's home or weaken her will to leave, Katelyn slipped into the night. The mist of the rain enshrouded her, and she ran toward Medora, dodging the gathering pools that puddled the empty streets.

Katelyn mentally lambasted Luke Stanton more than once during that long, sleepless night. He inhabited her thoughts and visited her dreams, keeping her awake more surely than a pot of thick black coffee could ever have done.

The rainstorm intensified, driving hard pellets of water against the house and beating out nature's age-old rhythm on Katelyn's window.

She felt all angles and sharp edges trying to fit her tense body to the flat expanse of mattress. Tossing the bedclothes into a jumble, she then kicked angrily at the twisted bedding tangled about her feet. Plumping the pillows against the headboard, she even tried to sleep sitting upright. But nothing worked. Her internal storm and the external one would not let her rest.

Luke, Randy, and the Deity Luke had so much confidence in kept tumbling through her mind like pebbles in a rock polisher, clacking against her common sense, her emotions, and each other until all should have been worn smooth.

The thoughts of God troubled her most of all. Randy, after all, was history. Luke, as much as she hated the thought, could become just a memory as well. But God! How would she deal with an intangible being whose very name humbles nations?

Fortunately for Katelyn, dawn could not break through the gray clouds, and at the time she usually rose, she slept.

"Katelyn? Katelyn? Are you still sleeping, honey?" Her mother's voice pierced her slumber.

"Yeah. What time is it?" She stretched stiffly and reluctantly, feeling the effect of her nocturnal thrashings.

"Nearly noon."

"Noon!" Katelyn bolted upright, tossing off the covers. "I'll be late for work!"

Her mother's voice drifted through the door again. "No work today. That's why I let you sleep. Everything is shut down. There's so much water everywhere they don't expect anyone at the chateau. The Visitor's Center will just send them away if they do come. There's six inches of water on Main Street. I baked caramel rolls if you want one."

"Be right out." Katelyn pulled on a pair of short cargo pants and a splashy red and white cotton blouse. At least her clothing could be bright even if her mood and the day weren't. The color red and the flames of her hair always set up such a clash that perhaps no one would notice her pallor.

"Coffee?" Mary poised the pot over an empty cup.

"Please. The rain kept me awake last night. It pounded away like a trip hammer."

"Hmmmm. Not to mention the thunder and lightning. I must have jumped a foot at one loud crack. I would have sworn it came down in our kitchen."

"Where's Daddy?"

"Out looking around. Where else? He'll track home in muddy boots looking for something to warm his insides any minute now."

"Doesn't he have to work today?"

"He's not on duty. But that doesn't mean a thing. He works more during his vacations than most people do on the job."

"But he loves it, doesn't he?"

"More every year. This country is addicting, I think—especially to an outdoorsman like your father. I've heard it described as ugly and sinister, but I don't think there's a place more beautiful."

"Even in the winter?" Everyone in Medora complained about the arctic winter weather.

Mary chuckled. "Even in the winter. We like to complain, but even when everything is practically paralyzed out here, it's beautiful. Sort of a magnetic desolation." Then Mary smiled self-consciously and her hands fluttered to her cheeks. "My! Don't I sound poetic today!"

Katelyn grinned into her coffee cup. She was beginning to come to life again after her horrible night. Things seemed more in perspective here in the light, at her mother's table.

The rain showed no signs of ceasing. Bored and restless, Katelyn scanned the bookshelves in the living room for a diversion. They were filled with the writings of Theodore Roosevelt, his quotations and biographies. Picking out an old volume crusty with age and disuse, she eased into the corner of the couch. She liked to read about the young Roosevelt, for even then he showed distinct signs of the man he was to become.

Her eyes traveled through the pages, skimming for some unfamiliar tidbit.

The quotation sprang out at her, startling her with its simple profundity. Roosevelt was speaking of his father. "He certainly gave me the feeling that I was always to be both decent and manly, and that if I were manly enough, nobody would laugh at my being decent."

Luke was like that, both decent and manly—an unusual combination in this day and age.

"What are you reading, Katelyn?" Mary wandered into the room, wiping her damp hands on the front of her apron.

"About Teddy Roosevelt."

"Good reading. That man was a real fireball of energy and intelligence. We're lucky to have him as a part of our history. He's the only U.S. president North Dakota can claim."

Katelyn nodded distractedly. Roosevelt wasn't foremost on her mind at the moment. "Mom, do you know Luke Stanton very well?"

"Fairly well, I'd say. He's a very polite and friendly young man. He doesn't make me feel like I'm in my dotage. I appreciate that. Fifty isn't exactly dead and gone, in spite of what some young people think!" Mary settled on a corner of the piano bench and studied her daughter. "Why?"

"Some things he's said have made me...think."

"He's a very handsome man." Her mother cut through to what she obviously thought was the heart of the matter.

"True. But he...well, he's *more* than that."

"A Christian, you mean?"

Katelyn was startled to hear her mother voice it so frankly. She nodded dumbly.

"He's set your father to thinking, too. And as a result, me. Ben admires Luke. He's just what Ben would have wanted in a son. The only thing about him that Ben's had trouble accepting is this Christianity thing. So your dad's been doing some reading himself. Even we old folks can learn a new trick or two."

So Luke's faith has even touched my parents!

But Mary went on, more to herself than to Katelyn. "When Luke's around it's like there's a glass barrier between them. Nothing you can see, mind you, but there. And whatever it is, Ben's not happy about it."

The slant drilling. Her father's suspicions were causing him as much pain as they were Katelyn. More and more she believed that Luke could not be involved. Not and talk as he did of God. But until that

156

was resolved, neither she nor her father would rest easy.

"You know," Mary continued, glad to have an audience for her speculations, "what Dad likes least about Luke is also what he likes most."

"I think you'd better explain that one, Mom."

"Luke's drive. His ambition. His motivation."

"What doesn't Dad like about that?"

"Luke's motivation is his love for God. He's all the good things your dad admires because he's a Christian. Your Dad's denied God for so long it's hard for him to see Him in action now. But Ben will settle it in his mind in his own good time. I don't doubt that." Mary, hearing the clamor of the oven timer, stood up. "Sorry I interrupted your reading, honey. Now I'll be quiet."

Katelyn returned her eyes to the page, but the words were a squirmy blur.

Motivation. Decent. Manly. Luke got his impetus, his inspiration, from Scripture, from God.

Curious and oddly compelled, Katelyn stood and walked to the bookcase. She scanned the shelves until her eyes fell upon her grandmother's Bible.

The afternoon slipped away as Katelyn read verse after verse on the fragile onionskin pages. Spidery notations told her someone in her family had been here before, seeking the same clues for life. And her heart swelled with excitement as she repeated the ancient lines. This Book *could* speak to her! But with every answer came a thousand questions.

She snapped the Book closed. Luke could help her with this!

As soon as she'd made her decision to seek him out, a weight slipped from her shoulders. She'd have to apologize for her behavior of last evening. When she explained the confusion and hunger she'd been living

157

with, she could ask him what all these wonderful words really meant—assuring peace and joy and love and salvation.

Excited as she hadn't been in a long time, Katelyn reached for a slicker and hat. Even the rain couldn't dampen her spirits. She was too close to having answers for questions long unasked.

Nothing was going to keep her from the cabin now. She needed to talk to Luke.

Chapter Eleven

The rain had come hard and fast. The smooth soles of Katelyn's shoes provided no traction in the muddy gumbo of the streets. It would take her forever to get to Luke's this way. Turning back, Katelyn peeked into the old pickup truck parked off the edge of the driveway. The keys dangled from the ignition.

She climbed onto the high seat, shaking droplets from her head and shoulders onto the scarred and battered cushion. Her father had purchased this old truck when she was a child and had never been able to part with it.

"This baby travels through mud and muck like no other vehicle I've ever seen. She's worth keeping for that alone," her father had said. Well, Katelyn would see.

The shabby little vehicle sprang to life with a single twist of the key and Katelyn's foot heavy on the accelerator. It had been some time since Katelyn had driven a standard transmission, but she ground her teeth in tune with the gears until she found reverse and backed onto the road.

Hiccupping forward, Katelyn crossed town and headed for the hillside and Luke's cabin. Water rushed down the slopes and pooled everywhere, coming too quickly for any natural drainage to occur. The water was thick and ashy, reflecting the sour complexion of the clouds.

Luke's cabin was dark, the windows staring like vacant eyes into the gloom, but a feeble light came from the tack room. Katelyn lurched to a stop in front of the building.

"Luke? Luke, are you in here?" she called from the doorway. The grumbling clouds might have obscured her arrival, and she didn't want to startle him. She had enough startling things to discuss with him later.

"Can I help you...? Oh, hi, Katelyn!" It was a familiar voice that met her, but not Luke's.

"Carlton? Carl Thureen? What are you doing here?" Carl had graduated from high school with Katelyn and ranched not far from Medora.

"I could ask the same thing about you. But then again, I did hear you were home for the summer. How's it going?"

"Where's Luke?" Katelyn had no time for small talk.

"Wish I knew. I came to ask him about buying a horse, and the place is empty...."

Just then a new sound reached them.

"Luke? Luke? Is that you? I was worried...." Katelyn's voice trailed off in disappointment. "Oh, I thought you were Luke."

"Hi, Bobby. Where's your bossman?" Carl inquired.

Bobby was a sixth-grader who helped Luke during the summer months, saddling horses, matching riders to mounts, and rounding up stray tourists whose horses wandered off the beaten path.

"I don't know."

"You don't know? Have you checked the cabin?"

"That's the problem, Mr. Thureen. He didn't come

160

home last night. I waited here till almost midnight. Then Ma came to fetch me. His bed hadn't been slept in this morning."

A nauseating lump was forming in Katelyn's stomach. What was going on here, anyway?

"Luke was worried about some horses. That big black he bought in Dickinson and a couple of others got away through a break in the fence. He put down most of his savings on that new stallion 'cause he wants to hire him out for stud. So he didn't want them out in the bad weather. He went out looking on one of the trail horses. That was about an hour after the rain started. And he isn't back yet." Bobby's voice cracked with fearful devotion. The alarm in his eyes told her Luke had endeared himself to the boy.

"Where could he be, Carl?" Katelyn heard her own voice but barely recognized it, high-pitched with alarm.

"I don't know, but I think we'd better find out. I can't think of many safe places in the Badlands in weather like this." Carl's features had sunk into somber lines, and he chewed on his lower lip.

"Luke took a gun and his rain poncho," Bobby offered. It was obvious he'd comforted himself with that scrap all night. "I was just going for help. I would have gone last night, but I was afraid Luke would think I was a big baby, worrying about him and all. But this morning..."

"Is your father home, Katelyn?" Carl asked.

"He wasn't, but Mom said he was uptown. I can call around...."

"Phones are out. You'll have to go looking for him. Maybe he has some suggestions. This rain is making the trails impassable. I just hope Luke didn't cross the river. It's swollen to the edge of its banks. I'll stay here

161

and help Bobby saddle some horses. Ben and I can go out and look for him.

"Saddle one for me, too."

Carl's eyebrows shot up under the brim of his hat. "*You*, Katelyn?"

"Me. I'll go find Daddy and be right back."

Fortunately for Katelyn, Ben was just making a dash for his car when she drove down Medora's Main Street. She slammed her foot onto the brakes and skidded sideways toward him, stopping only inches from the rear fender of his car.

"What in tarnation is going on here, Katelyn Ryan? What makes you think you can…?" Then, seeing the stark terror on her face, his voice changed. "Kitten? Darlin'? What's wrong?"

"It's Luke, Daddy. He's missing. He went to look for some horses in the hills and never came back. He's been gone all night. Something must have happened to him.…" Katelyn could no longer distinguish tears from rain running down her cheeks.

Ben swung into the pickup beside her. "Does anyone else know?"

"Carl Thureen was up at the stables looking for Luke. He and Bobby are saddling up some horses."

Ben nodded approvingly. "Carl's a good rider, and I know this area like the back of my hand. Between us we should find Luke. No use getting more people excited yet. It's too dangerous for just anybody to go riding through these hills. A horse can't keep his footing in slime or predict a washout."

A leaden ball settled in Katelyn's stomach. It all sounded even worse when her experienced father detailed the possibilities.

Ben continued. "Maybe, just in case, we should call an ambulance. Luke will be madder than hops if he's

162

all right, but if he's hurt, it would be nice to have one on hand."

"The phones are out."

"Blast. I forgot." Then Ben's eyes traveled over his daughter. "But Luke won't need medical help anyway. He's tough, and he knows horses and these hills."

After stopping just long enough to tell Mary what had happened, Ben continued. "I'm surprised he took off at the beginning of a big rain."

"His new horse was missing. The black stallion."

Ben's eyes darkened as he nodded. "Luke put down big money for that horse. Wonder where he got it."

That slant drilling scheme came up even now. Katelyn brushed it away like a pesky fly. "Bobby told me he'd spent his whole savings. He wants to use the horse for stud. That makes sense, doesn't it?"

"Then it's one of the few things that does." Much to Katelyn's relief, Ben dropped the subject. They pulled up at the stables just as Carl led three horses from the barn.

"What's he got that extra horse for? Luke?"

"No, Daddy. For me."

"You? Are you crazy? You've been on a horse so little in the past few years, you probably don't remember how to ride. I can't take you out with me."

"Then I'll go alone."

Katelyn's jaw stuck out with typical Ryan determination.

"Then don't go slowing us up or falling in a puddle."

Secretly, Katelyn was quaking, but outwardly she was the most composed of the small group.

Carl was shouting useless orders, Ben nervously checking and rechecking the cinches, and Bobby fighting back tears. Finally Katelyn took matters into her own hands.

"Well, let's get on with it then. This isn't a tea party." Ben and Carl shot her looks of grudging admiration as she reminded herself to fall apart later, in the solitude of her own room—or the haven of Luke's arms.

They moved out across the slick earth leaving Bobby behind. His small thin silhouette in the tack room's open door gradually diminished and disappeared as they wound their way into the countryside.

The hills wept rivulets of watery tears and Katelyn was drenched to her very core. Her rain poncho proved useless against the driving pellets. The persistent wetness insinuated its way through the fibers of her clothing and settled in to chill her skin.

The horses slipped and skidded on the slimy clay slopes and fought valiantly against the sticky gumbo clinging to their hooves. Katelyn mentally divided her job into two parts. The first was scanning the gray hills for signs of Luke. The second was hanging on.

Her legs quivered and ached with the unaccustomed clutching of her thighs to the saddle. She almost gasped in relief when she saw her father and Carl had pulled up in front of her.

"Well, what do you think?" Carl shouted across the noise of pelting rain.

"If he could, I know Luke would get some shelter. He could be tucked under some brush or a tree and easy to miss."

Carl nodded, and for the first time since they had started out, Katelyn saw his eyes. Fear in Bobby's eyes had been acceptable. The fear in Carl's was not. Then he spoke.

"We've got to find him. I've been out in this stuff less than two hours, and I'm chilled to the bone. If he's

164

hurt and been lying out here all night…" Carl's voice trailed away.

Katelyn threaded her fingers through the reins and made ready to start out again. There weren't many hours until nightfall on a dreary day like this one. They'd have to hurry.

Desperately she wished she could do more. Luke would pray. But she didn't know how.

Quagmires sucked greedily at the horses' hooves with great, hungry slurping sounds. Katelyn could feel the hardy trail mount tiring beneath her, slogging patiently through the mire. Her eyes and her shoulders ached with the physical strain of the search and the psychological fear of losing the person who had become so dear to her.

She scanned the landscape. All was gray today, accented with the green of new life springing from the nourishment of rain. The rocks were washed clean of the year's grimy accumulations. To her left was a scraggly shrub drinking up the rain she was so busy cursing. A green shrub and a shining black rock.

A black rock? Katelyn couldn't remember seeing anything of that size or sheen in these hills. As she nudged her mount forward, she saw it wasn't a rock. It was a horse. A dead horse. Luke's horse.

Fighting the gorge rising in her throat, she edged her way closer to the animal as she shouted for her father. Partially sheltered by the shrub was another leg, this time a human one.

"I've found him! I've found him!" She felt the screech tear at the tender lining of her throat. And the leg never moved.

Ben and Carl were upon her before she could muster the courage to slide from her horse's back. She swung a stiff leg across the saddle and dropped like a dead weight to the ground.

Luke's prize possession. The animal's glassy eyes followed her movements unseeing. A bullet hole glistened in the smooth arch between the eyes. Swallowing deeply, Katelyn knelt beside her father and Carl, their shoulders blocking Luke's face from her line of vision.

"He's alive. I can see him breathing." Carl's voice burst into her consciousness.

"Horse broke its leg in this mire. No wonder. I'm just surprised it didn't happen to us."

"Luke must have put it out of its misery several hours ago. *Rigor mortis* has set in."

"Sometime last night, I'd wager. Looks like he crawled in next to the carcass to get what little shelter he could. Here, Ben, help me roll him over. Luke? Luke…"

A pained hiss rolled across Carl's lips, and she peered over his shoulder.

Luke's head rolled to one side as Carl moved him. An angry wound split his forehead over one eye. He was so ashen and still, Katelyn began to doubt he was alive after all.

Then he began to move. The rain, spilling across his face, disturbed his deep, unhealthy slumber. He'd spent the night with his face buried against the stiffening body of the horse to protect himself from the unceasing downpour, and now the water had found him again.

He struggled to sit. Ben and Carl each took a shoulder and supported him carefully.

Katelyn watched Luke's eyes focus and clear. They grazed an unbelieving trail across her toward Ben before he tried to speak.

"Where…how…?" Luke brushed a confused hand

across his forehead, breaking open the clotted gash over his eye. Blood began to pour into his eyes, blinding his vision. He straightened his neck and tried to stretch, his every movement slowed by stiffness and the weight of sodden clothing.

"We've got to get him back to the cabin. Is there something around here to make a pallet?" Leaving Katelyn with Luke, Ben and Carl looked for branches to devise makeshift transportation.

Luke's shoulders rested on Katelyn's lap. He felt cold as a block of ice. She staunched the flow of blood from his head wound with a crumpled napkin in her pocket and crooned comforting gibberish into his ear.

He twisted his head toward her and spoke. "Horse broke its leg." The effort cost him dearly, and he leaned even more heavily across her lap.

"I know, Luke. It's all right. You did the right thing."

"Can't move my leg either."

Her eyes traveled down the soaked blue-black denim line of his jeans. His right leg was rigid and twisted a bit oddly. Before she could respond, he spoke again.

"Just don't shoot me."

She didn't know whether to laugh or cry. She'd lost her sense of humor for the moment, but by some mighty feat Luke had retained his. Then Ben and Carl were upon her.

"We'll have to strap him to your saddle, Katelyn, and lead the horse out. You ride with Ben, and I'll take the horse."

"But he's hurt!"

"No other way, honey. We can't find enough long branches for a pallet. And nothing else can travel through this slime. As soon as he passes out from the pain, we can move faster. Let's get going."

It seemed an odd comfort, hoping Luke would slip into unconsciousness. But he didn't, not until they were very near the stables and his horse stubbornly paused to graze on an outcropping bush. The offending growth stabbed Luke in the leg, and Katelyn saw him slump deeply in the saddle. He would have tumbled to the ground had it not been for the rope looped around his waist, over the saddle horn, and under the horse's belly.

Bobby was again standing in the door of the tack room when they arrived. He did an excited jig about the sopping foursome as they dismounted and untied Luke from the saddle.

"You found him! You found him! Is he okay? Is he okay?" Bobby seemed determined to repeat his questions until they were answered. Luke looked far from all right as Ben and Carl half-dragged and half-carried him into the house.

Katelyn's grip tightened about the tiny parcel she had picked from beneath the dead horse's belly when Carl and her father moved Luke. She pulled the sodden pocket Testament from her slicker and studied it carefully.

The pages were melted together with moisture. He'd had something to cling to in those long hours huddled against the belly of his dead horse. Now Katelyn desperately needed something to cling to as well.

The commotion from inside the cabin drew her there. Bobby had unfolded the couch to make a bed and was building a fire in the fireplace.

Ben and Carl were pulling the saturated clothing from Luke's body. Katelyn, her eyes on Luke, tripped on his discarded boots. One toppled with a soggy thud, and water dribbled across the wood floor.

"Prop him up, so I can get his shirt off." Ben tugged

168

at the clinging arms of Luke's shirt. "This stuff is plastered to him like wallpaper. We'll just have to peel it away."

Katelyn watched, her eyes round, as they stripped off the saturated layers. Luke was beginning to shiver. The thick, well-defined muscles of his chest quivered involuntarily as he began to warm. Katelyn flexed and curled her fingers, aching to lend some warmth to the golden expanse, but she remained rooted to the spot.

"Katie, darlin', go get all the towels he's got in his bathroom. We've only got a few left here. We must have brought an inch or two of rain inside on his back. And look around to see if he has a heating pad or a hot water bottle. Anything to help warm him up."

Relieved to have a task, Katelyn ransacked every cupboard in the bathroom. She found herself running exploratory fingers over the intimate, insignificant items that such rooms hold. Luke's toothbrush. A neatly stacked stockpile of unopened soap. His razor. Horse liniment.

She smiled at the last item. The dividing lines between stable and house had blurred somewhat. Suddenly she found herself shuddering with deep, wrenching sobs. Luke's beautiful horse was gone.

How it must have hurt him to put the stallion out of its misery. So pitiful in death, muddied and rigid, it hadn't even been a shadow of the prancing majesty they had both so admired. It had hardly looked like the same animal.

"Katelyn! What are you doing in there? We need more towels."

Ben's voice broke through her introspection. Hurriedly, she pulled open the last closet. Success! Folded neatly and resting on the shelf at eye level were several blankets, one of them equipped with cords and controls. She scooped the whole pile into her arms and took them to her father.

"I found an electric blanket, Dad. Will that help?"

"Good. He's shivering from stem to stern. You didn't see a thermometer in there, did you? His internal temperature is probably down a couple of degrees. Trouble is, if he gets as sick as I expect he will from his bout with the weather, it's going to shoot up before the night's out."

She shook her head. She hadn't even seen an aspirin on the shelf. Luke obviously wasn't the sickly sort.

Ben and Carl had Luke in bed. Katelyn's toe brushed the soaked heap of clothing at its foot. Luke had curled unconsciously into a fetal position, wrapping around himself for what body heat he could generate. The tight muscles of his back relaxed as Ben and Carl piled the cache of blankets across him. Topmost was the electric blanket, turned high.

"Think his leg is broken?"

"No. Badly sprained, though. He was moving it a few minutes ago. And I think we'd better leave that head wound alone until the doctor gets here."

"I don't know if we're doing the right thing for him or not," Carl finally ventured, "but it's the best we can do."

"I'll go find a two-way radio to call on or drive into town and pick up the doctor. You'd better get yourself on home, or your wife's going to think you got stuck in the mud," Ben instructed. "Katelyn and Bobby can stay with Luke until I get back."

Nodding, Carl struck for the door. "Give me a call when the lines are repaired. I'd like to know how he's doing."

Katelyn had turned back to Luke before Carl disappeared through the cabin door. She barely heard her father follow him, so intent was she on memorizing the planes of Luke's face in repose.

The taut angles of his cheeks softened as the warmth of the room and the heavy heat of the blankets seeped into the innermost core of his body, finally offsetting the numbing chill that had settled there.

She hardly dared to breathe for fear of disturbing him and eased herself into the chair at the foot of the bed. Waving Bobby away when he poked his face to the window, she sat staring at the motionless body before her.

More than ever, she wished she could do something. Tiredly, she closed her eyes, and when she opened them, they fell on the Bible resting on the lamp table by her chair.

Here was something she could do. Amateurish and inexperienced as she was, perhaps she *could* pray.

As her fingers surrounded the bound volume, it fell open to the book of Matthew, and she began to read. She read the confusing "begats" of the ancestors of Christ, of King Herod's vile order to kill the boy babies in his land, of John the Baptist, of Jesus. And at the end of the fourth chapter, her attention was riveted on a single verse. "Then His fame went throughout all Syria; and they brought to Him all sick people...and He healed them."

And He healed them.

Dropping her chin to her chest, Katelyn put forth the first petition of her life. Wordless and timid, but sincere. And as she raised her head again, it was as though a weighty burden had lifted from her life as well. Somewhere in that small, tentative prayer, she had discovered a new friend, someone to heal Luke—someone to heal her.

Now she was more eager than ever for Luke to

awaken. He could explain this lighthearted excitement bursting within her. Luke could explain everything.

Luke.

He was beginning to squirm under the covers. The mound of blankets rose and fell as though a mole were burrowing in shallow earth. He moaned and rolled over onto his belly, finally stretching out of the tightly woven ball. He stretched diagonally across the bed and threw a protective arm over his eyes.

The covers fell away from his shoulders revealing the golden skin of his back. A three-cornered nick distinguished his right shoulder. Katelyn gave in to the urge to run a light finger across the whitened scar.

Standing, she grazed the supple skin with first an index finger, then more insistently with the entire palm of her hand. Luke was burning up.

The feverish heat of his body surprised her. She ran a gentle hand across his forehead and found her fingers tangled with the sweaty strands of his hair. First he'd been too cold. Now he was too hot. Just as her father had predicted.

Purposeful, Katelyn hurried to the kitchen for a pan. Filling it with tepid water, she carried it to his side. She could sponge his forehead until the doctor arrived. She had to keep busy. Luke's restless thrashings were intensifying.

He had flipped from his stomach to his back by the time she returned to his side and had kicked a good portion of the blankets away. A fine feverish mist shrouded the upper half of his body.

"Anything I can do?" Bobby poked his head around the corner of the door.

"Come inside. Don't leave that door open to give him another chill."

"Sorry." The boy scurried inside. "How is he?"

172

"He's running a fever. Did you see any sign of my father?" She sponged Luke's neck and shoulders, unmindful of the seeping dampness on the bed beneath him.

"No. But he told me that if he couldn't rouse somebody on a radio, he'd just drive somewhere and get a doctor if he had to kidnap one."

Katelyn nodded, appreciative of the boy's chatter. Luke was getting hotter instead of cooler, and he'd begun to cough. She was becoming frightened.

"That doesn't sound very good, does it?"

The boy had a talent for understatement. The coughing tore at Luke's body, jerking it violently in his slumber.

Just when she thought she couldn't keep the fear back a moment longer, when Luke's fever and cough seemed to increase with every passing moment, a car pulled in next to the cabin.

"Mr. Ryan is here! And he's got somebody with him!" Bobby crowed in obvious relief.

The door swung open and the wind, the rain, and the doctor all came bursting through together. Ben followed, forcing the door shut against the gale. He quickly evaluated the situation and glanced wordlessly at the physician who was at work removing his rain gear.

The doctor took over Katelyn's place on the bed. His expert hands examined the hot forehead and the wicked gash over Luke's eye.

"Katelyn," Ben said, "why don't you go in the kitchen and see what you can rustle up in the way of food and drink? Some coffee and a sandwich, maybe. And some broth for Luke when he comes to. It's been a long day for all of us."

She glanced at her watch. Nine p.m. No wonder she

173

felt lightheaded. Nerves and hunger. Bobby followed her into the immaculate kitchen, and the two of them brewed strong black coffee and built a precarious stack of sandwiches from the meat and cheese in Luke's refrigerator.

"Think he's going to be all right?" Bobby inquired as he stuffed his third sandwich into his mouth.

"Of course." Katelyn hadn't meant to be so sharp, but that's how it came out.

Bobby looked at her sideways. "You his girlfriend?"

She started to shoot back a denial, but it stuck in her throat. "I *am* a friend."

"Does he tell you lots of stuff?"

She studied the boy curiously. This conversation was taking a very odd turn.

"Some 'stuff,' I suppose. Why?"

"Just wondering. He told me some stuff, and I was wondering if he'd told you."

"Oh?" Katelyn held onto the sound as she wondered what kind of "stuff" Bobby was talking about. It couldn't be about the horses. The only secret she could think of was...the slant drilling site. She tossed out some bait.

"You mean about the drilling?"

"Yeah! He did tell you then! He made me promise I'd never tell another soul. But he told you!"

Katelyn's heart lay heavily in her chest. "Bobby, did Luke tell you *everything* about the drilling?"

"Nah. He didn't want to tell me anything, but I wouldn't answer his questions until he did."

His questions? What questions?

"Questions? I didn't know Luke had any questions about...that."

"Sure. He wanted to know if I'd noticed anything funny going on by one of the wells. I ride up that way

174

quite a bit, and Luke figured I might have noticed something funny going on."

"And did you?" She felt as though she were picking her way through a minefield. She didn't want this conversation to blow up in her face, but she had to go on.

"Of course. The same as Luke." He paused suspiciously. "Say—he didn't tell you much at all, did he?" Bobby clamped his lips together in a determined press.

"Sorry. I didn't mean to have you break any confidences." Her contrite apology seemed to satisfy the boy, but their conversation was cut short by a yelp from the other room.

Bobby and Katelyn took a quick look at each other and bolted for the door.

Luke was awake and propped against a mound of pillows at the head of the bed. The doctor was bending over him, cleaning the gash in his forehead. Luke winced every time the cotton swab came near him.

"You're awake!" Bobby and Katelyn chimed together.

"And already a difficult patient," the doctor added tersely as he applied a white gauze patch to Luke's forehead. A dark forelock tumbled across the pristine square as Luke raised his head. He was pale under his tan, but conscious. And devastatingly handsome.

"I'm not trying to be." He gave a wan smile. He looked weak enough to be knocked off those pillows with one sweep of a feather duster.

"Good. Because I have some more work planned, and I'll need your cooperation," the doctor returned cryptically.

Katelyn heard Bobby give a sickly gurgle near her shoulder. Her eyes followed his gaze to the table where the doctor had spread his equipment—and two very large and intimidating hypodermic needles.

Luke's glance went to the same point, and Katelyn caught him rolling his eyes in mock dismay. He slid down on the pile of pillows until he was lying flat on his back. Then he mumbled, "I think it was easier being out in the rain."

Choking back a giggle, Katelyn excused herself and went back to the kitchen. She didn't care to be involved in this next scene. Bobby, no more eager than Katelyn to witness the next act, grabbed his jacket and headed for the porch.

Ben's voice drifted through the door. "You can come back inside now. I'm ready for a sandwich, and Luke wants to talk to you."

Luke was barely awake as she approached the bed.

"I gave him something to make him sleep. His leg's going to ache tonight," the still nameless doctor offered. "I'll come back tomorrow evening and check on him. If he's not better, we'll move him to the hospital, but he's opposed to that right now. I presume there's someone who can stay with him?"

Katelyn nodded. "I will." Then she noticed her father's raised eyebrow and the small grin turning up the corner of Luke's mouth. But the doctor nodded in businesslike agreement. Gathering his black bag and two sandwiches from the plate, he headed for the door.

"Take his temperature every couple hours or whenever he wakes up. If it spikes, call an ambulance somehow and bring him into Dickinson. Otherwise, I'll be back tomorrow."

Ben followed the doctor out the door, still gnawing on his own sandwich. He turned and called back. "I'll stop in after I tell Mary what's going on. See you later."

By the time Katelyn could devote her full attention to Luke, he was nearly asleep, his head nestled in the pillow, damp curls ringing his neck and twining about his ears.

"Thanks." The word was muffled in the pillow.

"You're welcome." Katelyn wound her fingers in between his dark curls. Then, suddenly, an idea came to her. She had to act quickly before the guilty feelings already budding had time to bloom and stop her.

"Luke?"

"Hmmm?" He burrowed deeper in the blankets.

"What's going on with that independent oil rig at the edge of the park?" If he were going to give anything away, it would be now, while he was drugged and vulnerable.

A muffled groan met her ears. "Did you see something, too?" He rolled over to look at her, fighting the sedative he'd been given. "I'm so sleepy, Katelyn, I can't…not now…." and his head tipped to one side. He was sound asleep.

And she knew no more than she had before. He didn't deny anything—or make any admissions. Somehow Luke was involved. Innocently? She certainly hoped so.

177

Chapter Twelve

"Katelyn, you can't stay here all night. I'll sleep in that chair. If Luke wakes up, I'll hear him."

"No, Daddy. I want to."

Midnight had come and gone when Ben returned to the cabin to check on his daughter. Luke was still sprawled face downward across the bed, deep in a drugged slumber. Katelyn sat rigidly in the chair, now pulled so near the bed that its corner touched the mattress. She leaned forward in the chair, supporting herself on her elbows, listening for every cough or suspiciously ragged breath.

"Then curl up for a nap. I'll stay here while you sleep a couple of hours. Then I'll go home, and you can sit there the rest of the night, perched like a vulture about to pounce. No matter how hard you try, you can't breathe health into the man, Katelyn. He'll have to do it on his own."

"Daddy?"

"What is it, kitten?"

"Do you still think Luke is involved in the directional drilling scheme?"

Ben sank wearily into a chair. "I don't know. I really don't. At the moment, things are pointing in that direction, but it just doesn't fit with the rest of the Luke we know."

"The part about being a Christian, you mean?"

"Especially that. If he's as sincere as I think he is, he wouldn't even be close to the scum that's pumping oil from under federal park land. But..."

"But what?"

"But *why* has he been seen with those fellows, Katelyn? There's got to be an explanation!"

Weariness overwhelmed even these disturbing thoughts, and Katelyn's head began to droop and then nod until sleep finally overtook her.

Several hours later, she awoke with a start.

"Oh!" Her stiff neck snapped upright.

"So you planned to sit here all night and not fall asleep?" Ben chuckled and stretched.

"What time is it?"

"Nearly four a.m. Think you can stay awake now if I go home for some shuteye?"

"I'm sorry, Dad. I didn't mean to sleep so long. Thanks."

Ben glanced over at Luke. "He's more restless now. The painkillers must have worn off. But I didn't see any point in waking him to give him more. He's been tossing and muttering for an hour or more."

"I can handle it now, Dad."

Ben nodded and rose. As he stood in the open doorway, he commented over his shoulder, "Rain's stopped. Should be a nice day today. See you later, kitten."

Katelyn only nodded, busy tucking blankets around Luke's shoulders. Just as she tucked the topmost blanket around him, he flipped onto his back, trapping her hand deep under his shoulder blade.

Not wanting to wake him, she leaned even nearer to

179

ease out the entrapped hand without disturbing his sleep. As her head tipped near his ear, he began to speak. "Sorry, buddy, I hate to do this, but there's no way out."

Startled, she pulled back. Was he awake?

"Don't be frightened, fellow. I'm sorry. I'm sorry." Luke was crooning gently in his sleep. Then he winced and started. Katelyn heard another muffled, "I'm sorry." Luke was reliving the moments when he'd put his beloved stallion out of its misery.

Katelyn slipped her hand out from under him and stood, studying him speculatively. Unpleasant thoughts were whirling in his fevered brain.

She settled onto the chair once again, almost hoping he'd wake from his tormented dreams. But, as it is in dreams, he slid from one to another in the space of a breath. Luke still had some things to work out in his dreamworld.

"I read the survey, that's why." Luke sounded indignant now. Katelyn stiffened. *What survey?*

She knelt beside Luke's ear and whispered softly, "What survey, Luke? Can you tell me?"

His eyes flickered open, unseeing, then closed again. For a moment she was afraid he would waken before she learned what she needed to know. But his body relaxed again, and he muttered into the pillow. "The geological survey...the oil survey."

"And what did it say?" She held her breath for his response.

He threw a long brown arm over his head, warding off the intruding questions.

Katelyn couldn't pull another word from Luke in his slumber. But Luke had *read* the geological survey concerning the oil. Wasn't that odd for a cowboy, no matter how bright? She began to wish she'd never prodded his dreams for information. Intruders sometimes found out things they didn't want to know.

"Run! Get outa here!"

Katelyn gasped in surprise as Luke bolted upright in the bed. The covers fell away from his long, tanned torso, still dotted with sweat. As she watched, his eyes cleared and focused, and he drew an unsteady hand across his forehead.

"Are you awake?" she ventured, not knowing when sleep left off and wakefulness began in his weakened state.

"Now I am. Did I just yell something?" He swallowed thickly, as though his mouth were full of cotton.

"You certainly did. You said 'Run.' Did you mean me?" She smiled. If he'd yelled, "Handstands," and meant her, she probably would have done it.

"I was dreaming about Ben Butler. The poor fella kept avoiding me. And then when I fell, he came and stood over me like he was apologizing. Dumb critter. I yelled at him to make him take off."

Katelyn stared at him, confused. Luke *sounded* coherent enough, but the words didn't make any sense.

"But Luke, the horse couldn't run. Its leg was broken. Don't you remember?"

"Not Ben Butler, too!" Luke's eyes took on a horrified glaze.

"Yes. Ben Butler—the horse you bought in Dickinson. What other horse was there?"

"No, Katelyn, Ben Butler is the horse I went looking for. The horse I was *riding* broke its leg."

Suddenly the puzzle pieces fit. Of course! Luke hadn't been forced to shoot the prize stallion after all!

"But I thought…I mean…you and the horse were lying there…."

"I took Blackie from the stable when I went out

181

looking." Luke's eyes darkened. "When he went down, I must have been knocked out, because when I woke up, Ben Butler was nuzzling me. *He's* the one I was dreaming about."

That's why it didn't look like the same animal. "And I thought you'd lost your beautiful new horse!" Katelyn breathed.

"No, but I lost a beautiful old one. Poor Blackie. I hated to do it." Then a puzzled frown flitted across his features. "How did you get them mixed up? Didn't you notice the saddle?"

She hadn't noticed anything but Luke. That horse could have been wearing ballet shoes and a combat helmet, and she wouldn't have known. But she couldn't tell him that.

Instead, she hung her head sheepishly. "We were pretty wet and scared. Guess I just didn't notice."

His silence made her raise her head. He was studying her intently, his eyes traveling methodically across her face. Then he reached a hand over the covers and grasped her fingers with his own.

"Thanks."

Warm, tickling emotion spilled through her. Her fingers took on a burning life of their own and curled into Luke's palm.

Smiling, he pulled her toward him and gently ran his fingers down the curve of her cheek to the softness of her lips. Then he captured them with his own. Her shoulder grazed his as she leaned toward him, hungrily searching for more of the tender, inviting warmth.

"Ben Butler's back! Ben Butler's back!"

They broke apart hurriedly as Bobby burst through the door. But it was too late. The boy's eyes were round as bicycle tires, and his mouth puckered into a silent O. "Sorry. I guess I should have knocked."

"Thanks for rounding him up for me, Bobby. Come on in. Katelyn was just welcoming me back to the world of the living."

"Are you all right?" The boy's Adam's apple bounced nervously. "How's the leg?"

"Stiff. But it's my hip that hurts."

Katelyn and Bobby looked at each other and giggled. No wonder, considering the size of the doctor's needles!

As his days of recovery passed, Luke began to try Katelyn's patience. Keeping him quiet was like keeping a grizzly bear in a thimble—impossible. One bright morning, when the rain was a memory except for an occasional puddle, Katelyn walked into the cabin carrying a small package.

"Whatcha got there?" Luke, fully dressed and looking suspiciously like he was headed for the stables, dived for the bed.

"Something to occupy you while you *rest.*"

"Awww, Katelyn! I've rested about as much as I can stand. It's wearing me out!"

"Talk to the doctor, then. He's the one who ordered you off that leg, not me."

"It needs exercise, not rest."

"Talk to the—"

"I know, I know, talk to the doctor, not you," he echoed. "Where's your dad?"

"Daddy? I don't know. He left home early. Someone called about six a.m. and he shot out of the house like a Fourth of July rocket. Why?"

"He called a few minutes ago and said he was coming up. Asked if you were here yet."

What was her father up to this morning? He'd been

acting like he had a secret these past few days, a pleas-ant one that made his eyes twinkle.

"I wonder what he wants. He's been jitterbugging around the house for days. He's got something up his sleeve."

"Looks like we'll soon find out what," Luke commented. His eyes were on Ben Ryan's form crossing the front porch.

"Top o' the mornin' to ya all!" Ben burst into the room. The screen door slammed and shuddered behind him.

"Same to you, sir. Don't think I've seen you this chipper in a long time."

"I've had things on my mind—thanks to you." Ben pointed an accusing finger at Luke.

"Me? What have I done?"

"That was my question exactly. It would have been a lot easier on me if you'd just *told* me what you'd been up to."

Katelyn mirrored the confusion on Luke's face. Had her father gone mad?

But as Ben spoke, the pieces of the puzzle began to fall into place. "Why didn't you tell me you were sus-picious of that well at the perimeter?"

A cautious look flitted across Luke's features. "You know about that well?"

"Now I do. Without any help from you, I might add. I had to piece it together from some sketchy talking you did in your sleep and what little Bobby had to say."

"Then they *are* pumping illegally?"

"*Were* pumping, you mean. We put a stop to it this morning. I might add that your name came up more than once."

"My name? Why?"

"That little truck driver lambasted you up one bluff and down another. He figured you'd turned them in."

Luke shrugged and settled himself deeper in the pillows at the back of the bed. "Wish I had. But I wasn't quite sure. Then I got hurt and couldn't do any more snooping. I didn't want my suspicions to tarnish a legal operation, so I thought I'd better keep my mouth shut until I was sure it was *illegal*."

"You almost got yourself in trouble, too, you know."

"Me? Why?" Luke's eyes widened in innocent amazement.

"We knew you were hanging around some of the truckers. Thought maybe you were involved. It took me a while to figure out you were as suspicious of them as I was."

Luke grinned. "I get myself into enough trouble without doing anything illegal, Ben. Look at me. In bed for a week—with a dictator for a nurse....Katelyn! What's wrong?"

Tears of relief and joy were streaming down her face. The last single question about Luke had been ripped away. And with it, the final vestige of her fear that she had fallen in love with another man like her former fiancé. Luke was exactly what he said he was and what he seemed.

Sniffling and with her eyes overflowing, she suddenly wished she could weep like women on a movie screen—and become more attractive doing it.

"I just *knew* you couldn't be involved! I just *knew* it!"

"You knew about this, too?" Luke leaned forward in amazement.

Katelyn nodded. As she did, she caught a glimpse of her father from the corner of her eye. He was tiptoeing silently backward through the screen door. He'd unwrapped that special secret he'd been hiding, and now he was going to let them enjoy the gift.

"But I just couldn't believe you'd be involved—because of your faith. I prayed and prayed it wasn't so."

"You what? You prayed?" Luke looked even more puzzled.

A smile like dancing sunbeams lit her features. "I did! I did, Luke. I prayed for you. I prayed for me. And God listened. I know He did. I thought I had to know *how* in order for it to work, but God could translate all my fumbling appeals. I knew that if He could do that, He could do anything."

Dumbfounded, Luke just stared at her. Katelyn burst into happy laughter.

"Look at the present I bought you!" With shaking fingers she tore into the bright package and gently placed the small volume into Luke's hand.

"A Testament?" He appeared baffled by the entire sequence of events, as if too much had happened during his illness and he could not absorb it all at once.

"I found yours in the rain. It was ruined, so I got you another. But I read it first. I hope you don't mind."

"Mind? How could I mind?" He fingered the tiny pages tenderly. "Katelyn, what can I say?"

Tears nearly kept them both from speaking. He was even more touched than she had anticipated.

"I'm the one who needs to say something. Thank you. Thank you for introducing me to something—no, Someone—who's going to help me straighten out my life. And thank you for proving that all men aren't the same—that some are absolutely wonderful."

"Come over here." His voice was gruff with emotion. He wrapped her in his arms, and she felt him bury his nose in her soft curls. His chest rose and sank deeply as he composed himself.

"Did you ever read what Teddy Roosevelt said about the Badlands?"

Katelyn stiffened. A conversation about Roosevelt was hardly what she'd expected next.

"He said lots about the Badlands, Luke." It was difficult to keep the disappointment from her tone.

Luke placed his index finger under her chin and brought her face close to his, so near that her bright curls brushed his shoulder. "He said that the romance of his life began in the Badlands. I guess now I can say the same thing."

Katelyn expelled the breath she didn't even know she'd been holding. But before she could speak, Luke continued, "I'm a great one for tradition, Katelyn. And I was just thinking, Medora is known for its red-haired brides. Do you think you'd want to be one? Of course, I'm not the Marquis de Mores or anything, but ....omph!"

Katelyn tackled him with abandoned delight, forgetting his injuries for the first time that week. When they came up for air, laughing, Luke waved her away.

"You shouldn't do that to a man in my condition, Katelyn. I may never be the same!"

"I certainly hope not!" She knew *she* would never be the same again.

As Luke bent to kiss her, Katelyn's mind drifted back over history—her own and that of this special place. And she smiled under Luke's seeking lips. The best of her dreams had come true. She'd found a man as handsome and brave as the marquis, as wise and decent as Roosevelt. But, most important and most unexpected of all, they now shared a love of God to grow in forever. Luke had fulfilled her dreams, her Dakota dreams.

We Love Hearing from You!

"This was my first Promise Romance ® and it certainly won't be the last."

A. M.—Murrells Inlet, SC

"I always recommend your books to my friends, both young and old."

M. P.—Philippines

"Your romance line is outstanding. I like the way you realistically portray the spiritual element while making your characters believable."

D. L.—Watertown, SD

"I read other books from different publishers but find Promise Romances ® the best."

B. P.—Altoona, AL

"Promise Romance ® is exactly what I've been looking for in a romance book."

D. R.—Brooklyn, NY

"I just finished my first Promise Romance ® and loved it…I am your typical romantic but I am also a Christian."

H. B.—Independence, MO

"Your books bring tears to my eyes but they are heavenly."

J. B.—Oshkosh, WI

"I have read 7 Promise Romances ® in the last 2 weeks and I have enjoyed each one."

J. F.—Baton Rouge, LA

"Keep 'em coming!"

L. C.—Alburquerque, NM

Promise Romances® are available at your local bookstore or may be ordered directly from the publisher by sending $2.25 for each book ordered plus 75¢ postage and handling.

If you are interested in joining Promise Romance® Home Subscription Service, please check the appropriate box on the order form. We will be glad to send you more information and a copy of *The Love Letter,* the Promise Romance® newsletter.

Send to: Etta Wilson
          Thomas Nelson Publishers
          P.O. Box 141000
          Nashville, TN 37214-1000

☐ Yes! Please send me the Promise Romance titles I have checked on the back of this page.

I have enclosed _____ to cover the cost of the books ($2.25 each) ordered and 75¢ for postage and handling. Send check or money order. Allow four weeks for delivery.

☐ Yes! I am interested in learning more about the Promise Romance® Home Subscription Service. Please send me more information and a *free* copy of *The Love Letter*.

Name _____

Address _____

City _____ State _____ Zip _____
Tennessee, California, and New York residents, please add applicable sales tax.

OTHER PROMISE ROMANCES®
YOU WILL ENJOY

$2.25 each

Dear Reader:

I am committed to bringing you the kind of romantic novels you want to read. Please fill out the brief questionnaire below so we will know what you like most in Promise Romances®.

Mail to: Etta Wilson
           Thomas Nelson Publishers
           P.O. Box 141000
           Nashville, Tenn. 37214-1000

1. Why did you buy this Promise Romance®?

   ☐ Author   ☐ Recommendation
   ☐ Back cover description   from others
   ☐ Christian story   ☐ Title
   ☐ Cover art   ☐ Other_____

2. What did you like best about this book?

   ☐ Heroine   ☐ Setting
   ☐ Hero   ☐ Story line
   ☐ Christian elements   ☐ Secondary characters

3. Where did you buy this book?

   ☐ Christian bookstore   ☐ General bookstore
   ☐ Supermarket   ☐ Home subscription
   ☐ Drugstore   ☐ Other (specify)_____

4. Are you interested in buying other Promise Romances®?

☐Very interested   ☐Somewhat interested
☐Not interested

5. Please indicate your age group.
☐Under 18   ☐25-34
☐18-24   ☐35-49   ☐Over 50

6. Comments or suggestions?

7. Would you like to receive a free copy of the Promise Romance® newsletter? If so, please fill in your name and address.

Name _____

Address _____

City _____ State _____ Zip _____

7389-7